D0891034

BEST

LESBIAN

EROTICA

2012

BEST
LESBIAN
EROTICA
2012

Series Editor

KATHLEEN WARNOCK

Selected and Introduced by

SINCLAIR SEXSMITH

CLEiS
PRESS

Published in the United States by Cleis Press Inc., 2246 Sixth Street, Berkeley, California 94710.

Printed in the United States.
Cover design: Scott Idleman/Blink
Cover photograph: Phyllis Christopher
Text design: Frank Wiedemann
First Edition.
10 9 8 7 6 5 4 3 2 1

Trade paper ISBN: 978-1-57344-752-2
E-book ISBN: 978-1-57344-769-0

"Never Too Old" by DeJay was published in *Lesbian Lust: Erotic Stories* (Cleis, 2010); "Rebel Girl" by Kirsty Logan was published in *Girl Crush* (Cleis, 2010); "My Femme" by Evan Mora was published in *Gotta Have it: 69 Stories of Sudden Sex*, (Cleis Press, 2011); "Bloodlust" by Giselle Renarde was published at Oysters and Chocolate; "When You Call" by Sharon Wachsler was published in *Bed: New Lesbian Erotica* (Harrington Park Press).

CONTENTS

For
Cheryl B. and Kelli

FOREWORD

I've never had such difficulty writing my foreword to this anthology. It's not from lack of having something to say; rather it's a matter of choosing the personal and historic landmarks as a jumping-off point for the remarks that you'll no doubt skim over before plunging headlong into this year's collection of erotica.

But when in doubt, say "thank you." And I'll start by thanking this year's judge, Sinclair Sexsmith, for the outstanding job she's done. I've known Sinclair for several years now; we've been between the same covers (in anthologies!), served on panels and shared evenings of readings, and in the last few months, I've grown to admire her more than ever for both her craft and eye as an editor, and her strength and courage as a friend and member of the community.

We had an excellent, invigorating exchange about the final choices for this volume, and even once we'd started the process, a detailed conversation (shouted, in a bar, on the night of the Lambda Literary Awards), that gave me more of an idea of how best to determine the stories to give her. Because we trust each other, and respect each other's opinion, we got the lineup that follows. As I say each month after my reading series, "Drunken! Careening! Writers!": I think this was the best one ever.

That Lambda Awards night, I ran into a friend in the East Village, and realized that one of the topics people were talking and blogging and tweeting about was the playwright Edward Albee's speech at the Lammies (he got a Lifetime Achievement Award). In his speech, he identified himself as a WRITER, before identifying himself as gay. There was a lot of criticism of that stance (and my friend commented that Albee had been saying it for many years), and I found myself wondering at the critique. After all, I realized, I identify as a writer first.

I was well into adulthood before I came out, and it was a process that took years and a square tonnage of denial that could power a small city. And yet, during all those years, I was a writer, and had a craft, and worked at it diligently. Even after I came out, which did wonders for my writing, I still paid first dues to the craft. After all, it's my chosen lifestyle.

A few years ago, I was in Chicago for a reading of one of my plays. It was Pride weekend, and I'd debated leaving New York on one of my favorite weekends of the year. I love to ride behind my sweetie on her motorcycle and wave to the cheering throngs, and stop for the moment of silence on Christopher Street, sometimes right in front of the Stonewall. And on the morning of my reading in Chicago, I got up and went to the venue, pausing as I saw a gaggle (an exaltation?) of drag queens on their way to Chicago's Pride Parade, and my footsteps turned to follow them. Until I realized: I have to go to my reading. And I went. That doesn't make me a bad queer, it makes me an artist, with all the accompanying ego and neuroses. And it's not likely we'll forget who we are: as Albee pointed out, Tennessee Williams was invariably referred to as a "gay" playwright while the likes of Arthur Miller are not referred to as "straight" playwrights.

Of course, identifying as queer first is no guarantee that everyone will love you. What moved me about Albee's speech at the Lammies were his passionate tributes to two friends and playwrights who had passed away the month before: Doric Wilson and Lanford Wilson. I quoted Doric's *Street Theatre* in last year's introduction, and talked about how his depiction of outliers in the queer community ruffled the feathers of what can now be considered its mainstream. I often heard chapter and verse from Doric about the people, many of them gay and lesbian, who'd prefer that he just keep his mouth shut, and not write about leather people and transpeople.

And what's all this have to do with *Best Lesbian Erotica*, Kathleen? (You might be asking). Well, I'll tell you. I looked at some of the reviews (both published, and personal reviews on Amazon and the like) for last year's volume, and found that everyone has her (or his) own idea of what is "best." For some, anything with a cock, whether real or purchased at the toy store, is not lesbian; for others, anything with BDSM is beyond the pale; and still others consider anything "trans" either MTF or FTM, to be "not lesbian" (or erotic). And then there are the folks who love the variety of the work, and give it two thumbs up, four stars, and a "hip hip hooray."

From within and without, people continue to nail themselves (so to speak) into boxes, paste the labels on the outside and try to find comfort in knowing exactly who they are and what they should and should not like.

Well, here's some dynamite to blow up the boxes.

This year's collection has a chronological arc to it. It starts with the story of two young girls in love: one embraces who she is, the other panics at the unknown. And so it goes through lifetimes: people fall in love some more, break up, have brief encounters, know each other better than anyone else, heal their wounds, have families, take vacations, find comfort, grow older, care for each other, continue their pursuits, and keep on keeping on.

I paid for a cable upgrade so we could watch the New York State Senate pass marriage equality in June 2011. That just seems to me to be one more step in the journey that recognizes me as an adult, a person with the maturity and responsibility (and the desire to take on the responsibility) of marrying, and having (and being) a spouse. Of course, there are many (including friends of mine) who see no need, have no desire to be defined as "married" and worry that the continued push for mainstream recognition takes away the identity (there's that word again) of queer people, and pushes them/us into predefined roles.

There are no prerequisites for enjoying this book. There will be no judgment, no identity checks, no right or wrong side of the column, no test afterward, no grades. Rather, you might want to pretend it's the first beautiful day of summer, and no matter what comes next, you're walking outside and it's warm and sunny out, and you feel great in your own skin.

As Sinclair and I were preparing this year's edition, we lost a dear friend and colleague. Cheryl Burke was a wonderful writer and a past contributor to *BLE*. We'll always remember and miss her. We'd like to dedicate this year's *Best Lesbian Erotica* to Cheryl and her partner, Kelli Dunham.

Kathleen Warnock
New York City

INTRODUCTION

I know what I want.

I knew exactly what I was looking for when I read the submitted stories for this anthology: dirty, smutty, smart about gender, smart about power, packed full of sex with the barest of necessary descriptions of setting and context, and, oh yeah, good writing. It doesn't have to be dirty in my personal favorite ways—with sultry accoutrements and costuming like stockings and strappy sandals, or with strap-ons and lots of fucking, or with blow jobs and dirty talk. I like stories where the characters are so turned on and lusty that I feel it too, even if it is not my particular kink or pleasure. I like stories with unique descriptions and rolling prose and insatiable narrators and rising and falling action. I like stories where I want to recreate the action for myself, when I am inspired by the delicious positions and settings and words.

Yes, and the words, let's not forget the words. That's what these kinds of books are all about, really. If you wanted a quick, easy turn-on, you could load up any of dozens of queer porn sites—there is no shortage of real, good queer porn out there. But for some of us that is too crass, and a well-done turn of phrase gets us swooning and biting our lips and rubbing our thighs together even more than a dirty video.

I didn't always know what I wanted. When I was coming out in the late 1990s, though there was a serious lack of queer porn in the video stores, there were plenty of people paving the landscape for what would become the blossoming queer porn of the 2000s. Diana Cage, *On Our Backs* magazine, Good Vibrations, (Toys in) Babeland, Annie Sprinkle, Susie Bright—and, of course, Tristan Taormino. It was Tristan's 1998 *Best Lesbian Erotica* anthology that clicked something into place for me, something I could no longer pretend wasn't there. I would hide the book in the back of the shelves at the bookstore where I worked, and I'd sandwich it between two others and sneak into the stock room to read when it was slow. I wore creases into the spine with Toni Amato's story, "Ridin' Bitch," and Karlyn Lotney's story, "Clash of the Titans." I was genuinely confused as to why I liked these stories so much. What was this effect they had on me? Why did I love them so much? *What did it all mean?*

I began to find other books, short stories and essays that helped move my budding baby dykery along: *Nothing But the Girl*—oh, swoon. That essay by Anastasia Higgenbotham in *Listen Up: Voices From the Next Feminist Generation. Cunt* by Inga Muscio. *Breathless* by Kitty Tsui. And the *Herotica* series, which was erotica for women before Rachel Kramer Bussel's prolific erotica editing career.

I bought one of the *Herotica* books at an indie bookstore— now gone—on Capitol Hill in Seattle when I visited one summer, before I moved there. But it proved to be too threatening to my boyfriend who, enraged one night after yet another argument about my sexuality, stabbed that book and two other lesbian erotica books with the wide-handled screwdriver that I'd used to masturbate with since I was a teenager.

These books are filled with three powerful things: Women who are empowered about their sexuality (which, by the way, does not involve men). Even the books themselves are threatening.

These books of lesbian erotica are not fluff. They are not nothing. They are not frivolous or useless.

For queers coming out and into our own, they are a path.

Fast-forward a few years and I'd managed to snag myself a lesbian bed death relationship, going out of my mind with desire and disconnection. I stopped writing, because the only thing I was writing was how miserable I felt, how much I wanted out of that relationship—a reality I wasn't ready to face. I decided that to work off my sexual energy, I would either go to the gym or I would write erotica. Well, I ended up writing a lot of erotica, rediscovering this tool of self-awareness and self-creation that had led me to smut in the first place, and I began writing myself back into my own life, back into the things that I hold most important: connection, touch, release, holding, witness, play.

My first published smut story was in *Best Lesbian Erotica 2006.* Between the time I wrote it and the time the book came out, I was beginning to end the bed death relationship, in no small part because I'd reminded myself of the value of the erotic, of my own inner erotic world, of erotic words. Between the time I wrote it and the time it came out, I started *Sugarbutch Chronicles,* (sugarbutch.net) which has carried me through these last five-plus years, often being my sanctuary, support circle, best friend and confidant.

Writing these stories, for me, has not been frivolous. They have not been nothing. They are not fluff or useless.

For me, they were a path back to myself when I got lost.

When I was lost, I had no idea what I wanted, aside from the basic daily survivals: work. Eat. Pay bills. Sleep. Shower. But when I wrote, when I connected with my own desire, I felt a little piece of me bloom and *become* in a bigger way. I felt more like myself.

I turned again to the great books of smut to help me find myself, to help me find a way back to a partner, a lover, a one-night stand—hell, even an hour with a Hitachi was sometimes enough. *The Leather Daddy and the Femme. Mr. Benson. Switch Hitters: Gay Men Write Lesbian Erotica and Lesbians Write Gay Male Erotica. Back to Basics: Butch/Femme Erotica. Doing It For Daddy.* And *Best Lesbian Erotica,* always *Best Lesbian Erotica.* I still eagerly buy it every year to see what the guest editor's tastes are, to see what the new trends are, to read the emerging new writers, to get my rocks off.

I rediscovered what I wanted through reading smut and writing it, through carving myself a path in connection with a lineage of sex-positive dykes and sex radicals and queer kinksters and feminist perverts.

After six years of writing and publishing erotica, I am thrilled to be a guest editor for the series which sparked me into queerness in 1998, thrilled to be choosing stories for the same series that published my first piece, "The Plow Pose," in 2006, and which helped spark me back to myself. It is so exciting to be contributing to this queer smut hotbed that Cleis Press has helped nurture all these years, and I'm so glad to continue to be part of it in new ways.

I know what I want now. And lesbian erotica, or as I prefer to call it, queer smut, has helped me not only visualize what is possible, but create a path toward getting what I want.

The stories in this book reflect my taste, my favorites, my

personal hot spots, certainly, but they are also the best-written stories from a large pile of well-written stories by some of my favorite authors, like Kiki DeLovely and Xan West. There are some less-well-known writers in here whose work you may not be familiar with, *yet*, but who will leave an impression on you, writers like Anne Grip and Amy Butcher. I found dozens of moments of signposts, signals directing me toward myself, words illuminating my own meridians of ache. With each story, with each act of lust, with each dirty command or submissive plea, I rediscovered my own want.

I hope you find some of what you want within these pages, too.

TOUCHED

Amy Butcher

"I know it sounds wicked strange," Sharon whispered, "but I think I've been touched." Her thick Boston accent pressed a staccato emphasis into the final word. She rocked slightly as she said this, her heart moving toward me then away. Something ached inside me with each pull.

Sharon had been agitated, so we'd skipped fourth period French, escaping to the top of the bleachers overlooking the football field. We sat cross-legged, knee to knee, the September sun purring against our skin. We were hunched forward like old women, the weight of our emerging adolescence hanging around our necks, bending us forward.

Years of Catholic schooling had indoctrinated me into the war of Good versus Evil but never had the battlefield felt so tantalizingly close. I swallowed hard, daring to lift my eyes toward hers. "By the Devil?" I asked, a mixture of terror and thrill sliding out alongside the words.

"No. By God!" she said, fingering first the hem of her own plaid school jumper then moving across to mine. "By God…"

she repeated quietly, taking a whole handful of the material and clenching it in her fist. I could feel her hand trembling through the fabric.

I sat back, relieved but confused. "Well, that's great, right? First off, God is definitely better than the Devil, right?" I struggled to understand her distress. "And second, this means you've been chosen. That's a good thing. I mean, Sister Abigail is always saying that only a few of us will be...chosen, that is."

Sister Abigail, our gym teacher and self-appointed guard against all things pleasurable, regularly prowled the hallways to admonish every possible transgression: from patent leather shoes (boys can see the reflection of your underwear) to makeup, from hand-holding to straddle-vaulting over posts (you might slip and damage your "womanhood"). Her mission: to eliminate everything that could lead us down the path of temptation.

"I know, it's supposed to be a good thing, but it isn't working out exactly as Sister Abigail described it." Her rocking continued. She placed one hand on my knee as if to counter her own movement.

"Ow!" I flinched, "That's the bruised one...remember? From when you tackled me the other day, jerk?" I stuck out my tongue toward her and gave her a wide-eyed stare. She lightened her touch in response but didn't let go. "So what do you mean 'isn't working out'?" I asked.

"Well, you remember how she said that if you were chosen then you'd feel the Holy Spirit inside?"

"Yeah..."

"That you'd feel a calling, almost like a stick up your butt making you stand super straight?"

"Well, yeah, although I don't remember Sister Abigail actually using the words 'stick up your butt...'"

"I know, that's just how I pictured what she meant."

We both laughed and leaned forward, touching forehead to forehead, before sitting back again.

"Well, anyway, that you'd feel some sort of buzz or zing, like being struck by lightning. That God would call you, whisper in your ear, that all of a sudden you'd rise above it all and become detached from the material world."

"Okay, I'm with you. Although I think if God ever decides to speak to me, he better speak up nice and loud. I'd hate to miss whatever he had to say but…" I turned and dug into my backpack for another piece of gum, held the packet out to Sharon, but she shook her head no. I chomped hard on the gum until it merged with the rest and I could blow a decent pink bubble that popped with a crack. "I mean, how would I ever hear him over this?" I asked, peeling the sagging bubble from my nose.

"Will you get serious for a moment?" Sharon said, placing her other hand on my other knee, nailing my attention in place.

"Okay, okay. I'm with you. So continue, my divinity incarnate. So what's the problem?"

"Well, I feel the zing and all, but by no means do I feel detached. In fact, just the opposite. It's like God has filled me full of warm honey, I feel it sliding and oozing all throughout my body. When I walk, each step feels like I'm touching an electric fence with my feet. It makes my whole body shake. The birds all look at me differently, like I'm one of them and they've been waiting and wondering where I've been. I want to hug all the trees, lick all the flowers, stick my nose in gym towels…I know it's crazy but everything just feels so rich and"—she paused, struggling to find the words—"makes me ache all over."

I looked at her, wondering if I was missing something. "So what's so bad about that? Seems like maybe dry old Sister Abigail just missed the juicy parts."

"I know, I thought about that…until the thought of her and

juiciness started to make me gag." We laughed again, bubbles rising from just below our ribs. "See the problem is, it's making me want things that I never heard of God wanting. It's firing me with a sweet hunger!"

"You mean like wanting a big old slice of hot apple pie, a scoop of vanilla ice cream melting and slipping and sliding off the side? Pretty sure Jesus never placed that order."

Sharon closed her eyes and I could see her thinking, her mouth watering so hard that she had to swallow, licking her lips with the extra wetness.

"Not exactly."

"Well, what then?" The bench was pressing hard into the bones under my butt. I unfolded my legs and let them drop to either side, straddling the rough board. Sharon's hands remained on my knees as she leaned forward conspiratorially.

"It makes me feel carnal," she whispered.

"You're just horny, dipshit!" I said diagnostically. "Totally normal, according to *People* Magazine. We're in our 'hormonal phase' so we're supposed to be lusting after guys. It's our duty!" I made it my business to stay educated—watching Oprah, reading *Cosmo Girl* and *Sugar*—and from all I could gather, we were supposed to be a cauldron of bubbling hormonal angst. Not that I was feeling much of that, but that's what the experts said. Seeing that this information hadn't calmed Sharon, I went straight to problem-solving mode, "So who do you think is cute? Kevin from Calculus?"

She shook her head. "I get all that you're saying, honest I do, but something about this feels different, much more important than Kevin could ever be." She paused and looked down at the narrow stretch of plank. Her thumbs pressed into the inside of my knees as she spoke across that bridge, "See, I feel all that... but I feel it toward you."

I seemed to have stopped breathing. I could feel a shallow pulse at the point where my butt hit the bench. In the distance, a bell rang and I could hear our classmates spilling out of fourth period. Her palms burned into my thighs, the heat at that point of contact chilling the rest of me.

"Okay." I swallowed, finding just enough air in my lungs to speak.

"Okay?" she repeated back, questioning.

"Okay," I repeated, trying to pull myself back into my head, back into the place where Oprah and *People* and Sister Abigail made everything make sense. "Okay, we can figure this out. I don't think you need to worry. I think you're just a little confused is all. You don't need to get all bent out of shape. I don't even think it's even God or anything 'touching' you. I *think* what we have here is a case of 'hormonal *verum obvius nefas locus!*" I said, proud of myself as much for my cleverness with Latin as for having navigated us back to the safe shores of generalized adolescent angst.

"Okay, eh?" she repeated, with a dare in her voice. Looking me directly in the eye, she slid her hands up along my thighs, her palms tracing each rise of crisscrossing muscle over bone as her thumbs traced an ever more dangerous course along the soft inner edge. A jolt of energy vibrated through my body when her wrists hit the edge of my jumper, gathering it like a wave, pushing it toward the surf line at my hips. "I can hear God whispering—I can, with all my soul—and he's telling me to do this."

She leaned forward even farther, lifting her hips slightly off the bench, the weight of her body pressing deep into the crease where my hips split thigh to pelvis, and pressed her lips directly onto mine. I tried to lean back but her hands were leveraging my spine, holding me upright. At first, her lips were hard, the tautness of muscles just beneath the flesh, insistent on my own. But then something softened, a fullness came to both our mouths and I relaxed into the gentle press. Like church bells, something called me, compelled me in, and I felt our lips part and the sanctuary of her mouth, my mouth, our tongues, come alive. Her thumbs slid deeper, pressing into the surprising wetness of the cotton fabric in my crotch and I felt myself arch forward to meet her. My tongue slipped into the bejeweled cavern of her mouth, teased with the dangerous sharp edges of her teeth, slipped gently across the pinkness of her gums. She took my lower lip between hers and pulled, swallowing me into her mouth, making me wish she could inhale all of me. She held my lip between her teeth for just a moment—danger and delight—and then released. I pulled back and gasped for a breath, staring at her wide-eyed. In my ears, a ringing silence. For a moment there was nothing but this: a feeling, a thing, a whole world that had sprung into being only seconds before yet had existed for all eternity.

"See?" she said, "You can feel it too! I think this is what God really is." Her moist eyes penetrated mine, offering an enormity that unhinged me. A bell rang marking the start of fifth period. A car alarm bleated anxiously from the parking lot. I teetered on the edge between worlds then tipped involuntarily. Even as the heat of her hands worked at my hips, I could feel a cold rod move up through my butt toward my head, filling the space she had just revealed in me. It pushed me upright, as Sister Abigail said it would, and forced Sharon's hands away. Pressing my skirt back along my legs, pressing the rough fabric back into my skin, I swung my legs across the bench and pressed them together to face the proper direction out toward the field.

Sharon stayed straddling the bench. She reached one hand toward my back, sensing the coldness that had filled me, but I shook it off. For a moment all was quiet as I rehearsed carefully in my head. The words that finally formed had such certainty that I knew they must be true. "This is not God working through you, this is confusion, the Devil, temptation...but this is certainly not God. We must be strong." I spoke all this toward the field, as if giving a sermon. I could imagine Sister Abigail nodding her affirmation from below. I knew Sharon would be devastated and ashamed; she'd need my compassion. I was holding God's will and he would guide us through this. I turned to face her finally, prepared to be strong enough for the both of us, even as I expected her to be in tears.

She was not.

She shook her head as she stared at me, those same brilliant eyes fiery and not the least bit ashamed.

"You're wrong! This is God...in all his glory!" she shouted, tossing her arms and gaze skyward in imitation of a holy-roller preacher. "And you felt it too! You felt the sound of the bleachers cheering vibrating up through your ass. You felt the heat from a thousand suns flow through my thumbs into your crotch. You felt the sky unfold on my tongue, the earth compost us through the press of our lips. You felt the world screaming with delight as we touched...and it scared the shit out of you!"

"Did not!" I said defensively and looked away. "Sure, it felt nice but it's not real, Sharon. It's not how it's supposed to be." She was quiet so all I could hear was the sound of my own breath, air flowing into the top of my lungs and then quickly back out again. I felt safe in this tiny container.

"Don't do this," she said, gently placing her hand on my back once again. This time I didn't shake it off. "You know, there are moments when we make choices that matter. Like when the football players are down there," she said pointing to the empty field. "Run or pass? Cut upfield here or over there? Dodge that tackle or run right through it? They never know for sure but they've got to choose, or the game chooses for them. You've got to trust your instincts too, or you'll never know what could have been." She pulled her hand away but I could still feel the heat of it searing through to my heart.

"You know now, you've felt it, but you've got to choose for yourself."

Sharon stood and shook herself nose to tail. She ran her hands down along her sides and across her butt, smoothing her jumper. Reaching down, she pulled up her kneesocks, smoothing them into place with a slow touch that made my belly ache hollow.

"This feeling, this is God, and nothing you or Sister Abigail or anyone else can say will make me feel any different." She grabbed her book bag and hopped down the bleachers then trotted back toward school.

Despite the heat of the fall day, everything seemed to wither and turn cold before my eyes. The green of the grass dulled and a thin haze washed the blue from the sky. The wood of the bench turned silvery and a splinter tore at the back of my leg. I sat steely, straight and still, watching her depart, yet inside I could feel some crazy longing still cupping the tiny ember she had ignited in my belly, protecting it until a day I too would catch fire.

HEARTFIRST

Kiki DeLovely

I don't know if I've ever witnessed anything more sexy than the intent and intensity in her eyes as she shakes her head no, slowly, side to side, when what she really means is "Fuck, yes." As though she's disbelieving of just how incredibly right it is. As if everything about me is so right that it's wrong. She takes her sweet time with that simple motion, as if she hasn't the slightest need to rush, despite the fact that other parts of her may be moving at much greater velocities. This apparent discord—between both the unspoken verbal and the pace of the physical—although seemingly misaligned, has a radical effect on my desire and even brings a sort of asymmetrical balance to my lust. It's allowing my passion to course wildly through my mind and, hence, my body—blood pounding like wild ponies through my veins and racing to deliver an aching throb of need to my cunt.

Though she's only known me a few months, she has this madness-making ability to cut me to my core with little effort.

We're surrounded by people waiting to be seated, but once

she's locked me in her gaze, all I can see is her. She takes a slow gander at me; eyeing my feet dangling on the last rung of the bar stool, trailing up my unladylike-positioned legs, fixing briefly on the lacy frill at the hem of my skirt (just long enough to lick her lips), before continuing upward. I wrap one of my patent leather heels around the back of her leg, innocent enough for public purposes, and pull her in a little closer. She closes her eyes, keeping them closed a little too long, and inhales deeply. A lecherous grin creeps across her mouth.

Leaning into my face, she pauses for several seconds—my heartbeat quickens in my clit—then makes her way to my ear. "You know that intoxicating scent of yours?" She waits just a beat for her rhetorical question to sink in and then continues, "I can smell you from here." My blush is hard and immediate, wondering: if she can smell my cunt in a crowd of people, who else can? And not caring in the slightest—feeling so gorgeous and cherished, so very pleased to please her with my scent alone.

I close the door behind us and she doesn't make me wait—thank heavens she doesn't make me. No romantic foreplay, no taking her sweet time, no making love to the goddess inside me. No. *Thank my luckiest stars*. No, she shoves inside me fast and hard. Faster. And harder. In and out. And in. And out. So many times, so fucking fast, I feel like I'm about to lose my mind. She knows I've been needing this too damn long to have to wait even a second longer to have her. So she pounds away at my cunt like she wants to break me in two, like a rapacious beast. And I thank the planets for aligning our worlds, calling forth this limitless ravaging.

She slides two of her free fingers into my mouth and I begin to suck. As I take them in, she grunts out of euphoria but still wants more. Plunging her fingers deeper down my throat, farther until I'm gagging, she leaves me trying just as hard to suck in air as I am willing more of her into me. I need more of her inside me. Obligingly, she adds another finger and takes me over and over again and won't stop after I've come once, twice, ten times. I lose count as I go out of my mind because she won't fucking stop, won't give me a chance to catch my breath, and I no longer care if I ever breathe again. She pounds me like she's furious at the universe for having kept us apart so long and she has to make up for all those lost nights of passion and sweat, the days of lust and pure bliss. I scream and writhe and cry out until I have no voice left.

It is only later, much later, quite a while after she's fucked me into oblivion, that she doubles back, retraces her steps, straps on her cock and takes her time. Slowly. So excruciatingly slow. She teases me to a point of so much more pain than her more violent actions could ever cause. I can't stand it, and it's only then that the tears start to rise. I can sense the first one welling in the corner of my eye, feel it catch in my throat, as she pushes into me so I can feel her going on forever. Do they even make cocks long enough that you can enter someone for days before hitting a wall and then withdraw for the following week? That is how long it feels like it's taking her to complete just one thrust. And the intimacy of it all is terrifying.

Just when I think it'll never end, she pulls out of me completely. She needs more of her inside me. So she smears thick lube across her entire hand, up over the knuckles, all the way to her wrist. I gasp in anticipation. I don't think I can take that much. But she proves me wrong; of course I can, four fingers are sliding inside me with ease and it's only a matter of seconds before she curves in her thumb and my pussy swallows her fist whole. Surprisingly quiet, I'd have expected screams to be tearing through my vocal cords now. Instead my diaphragm drops and I feel another opening up from deep inside. My rib cage expands and the back of my throat dilates as I wish it would when I deep-throat her cock. With the sharp twist of her wrist, she forces me to hit a pitch so high it's barely audible and I shudder as the orgasm echoes throughout my entire body. I feel a sound escape my chest, originating from lower still. The purest note that ever graced my lips, it sails right past them and floats up in the air. I imagine an opera singer hitting her highest note.

When I go in for her well-guarded pleasure, I'm careful. I read every last cue of her body; initiating as though it's about me. It isn't. It's about her. And us. But I'm good at making it seem like it's about me, at burrowing down somewhere sacred. I straddle her leg, grind my wetness against her thick thigh, moan in her ear about how good she's making me feel. As my tongue searches out her tragus piercing, she groans, and I can feel the reverberations making their way through her body. Knowing how erogenous this spot is—this tiny flap on the inside of her ear—knowing just what to do with it, is a powerful blessing. I take the ring between my teeth and tug, gently at first, and gradually work my way up to the point where it's either going to rip out of my teeth or her ear. It's one of my favorite ways to get her going. And one of hers.

Fucking her is a precious gift and I honor it, giving this inti-mate interaction the reverence it deserves. Her desire is tangled up in mine and it's impossible to separate the two. So I treat it as one. Make it about how she's getting me off while I'm edging my way in, down to the place inside her that calls for me and has been secured, sentry protected.

I move my hips in a tight figure eight and grind harder against her thigh, my juices gushing down her leg. She begins to grunt, "Oh, god..." but before she's even made it to the second word, I'm pressing my hip into her sex, and then she's adding a few syllables to a monosyllabic word, elongating the moan buried mid-*oh* while I draw out her pleasure. I wrap my mouth around her tit, my tongue delighting in how its efforts are rewarded by the feel of her nipple tightening, beginning to rise, pleading for more. I graze my teeth against it, reaching over to pinch and slightly twist the other one, bite down and then release. I bring my free hand to my lips and slip two fingers into my mouth. After a slow, deliberate extraction, they glisten prettily with my spit in the low light. I lower them between her thighs, as I watch her face. Easing my fingers into her ass first, working them against her G-spot until she's wordlessly begging me to slide into her cunt.

I delve in heart-first, straight down to a deep, well-hidden place. It scares her to no end, yet she grants me access. I know even before her tears surface, that I have found her inner aquifer. I have reached the place inside her and saturated it with love and all things beautiful, filling her in ways she didn't think possible; making it known that I treasure and adore all of her: her multilayered, gorgeous self; her powerful presence; her soft underbelly. No matter what the world has told her—I have delivered the message that she is strong and sweet and capable and good. And right. So very, very right. In all of who she is, in exactly how she makes her way through the world. She is praiseworthy and perfect. Which is not to say she is unflawed. There are fights in our future about toothpaste and how she wasn't there for me that time. But now, in this very moment, I am loving her so completely: every drop of her, prized and celebrated.

Something about her sparks my overwhelming need to protect her. She learns that she can stay here, nestled deep inside me. I'll squeeze my thighs together, holding her there, letting her fill me; I'll protect her from the outside world, not letting go. This is the place where she can cry and feel safe and overcome by it all and she can just be.

When the deluge gives way to drizzle and then dries into traces of salt on her cheeks, she runs her fingers between my lips. "So. Fucking. Wet." We float somewhere above this tangible world, we vibrate internally on a higher plane. Grinding against each other with a deep-seated fury, we amplify our envy of that other world where our souls are melded together without seams.

We writhe against each other, knowing we are stretched to our physical limits by each other's fists. We tear into each other, wanting to emulate the amaranthine nature of the other plane, where all of her is consumed by my sex, my soul. And her fervor devours me. Anything is possible; there are no laws of space or time. Our ardor set ablaze, we are a mess of twisted limbs, cum- and sweat-drenched flesh, pushing into each other with desperation. Where everything within and beyond our imaginations is granted. Deeply rooted in our bodies while pushing them to extreme edges. A chaotic whirlwind of *ohhhs* and *yeses* and begging and panting swirls around us as the floodgates give way to our frenzied lust and I'm clamping down on her fiercely, she's shuddering against me, we're crying out into the heavens, drowning in each other.

She takes me there.

REBEL GIRL

Kirsty Logan

He grabs a fistful of Evie's hair as he comes, pulling her close to his chest, whispering guttural curses into the side of her neck. His cock thrusts deeper into her, the ridge of the head rubbing her in just the right place, and she's so close, just one more...but he's already growing soft inside her, the condom puckered and wet.

She rolls off him, starts digging through her skirt pocket for her lighter and tobacco. He's wriggling back into his clothes, all elbows and legs in the cramped backseat. Evie rolls her cigarette expertly, fingers twisting and tightening like a magic trick as she looks out of the sweat-blurred windows at the car parked next to theirs. She hopes Katia is having more success with her man.

She can see vague shapes, knees raised and palms pressing out for balance. She imagines Katia, head thrust back and tits pushed out, sliding her slick cunt up and down on the endlessly hard cock. She tells herself she's only thinking these things because she's jealous, because Katia gets to ride her way to an explosive orgasm and Evie does not.

* * *

Katia has a mouth on her nipple and a cock in her cunt and she's moaning, "Oh, yes, oh, fuck, oh, yes." She's so close, almost cresting the wave, almost crowning the hill, and she feels the blood drain from her brain to her clit. He comes, grunting out an approximation of her name, and collapses with his head on her chest. She squirms under him, trying for release, but he's wrinkling away to nothing and the feeling has gone.

The backseat is sticky with sex and sweat. Katia feels around on the floor for her bra, wishing he'd wake up and get off her so she can get some air. The summer is humid, so hot she sweats in a bra and shorts, her skin always reddened and slightly swollen from the heat. Over the top of his head, the sweat-dampened curls behind his ear, she can see the car parked beside theirs. The windows are opaque with smoke, and it's stopped juddering on its chassis. Katia imagines Evie, sated and soaking into the leather fabric of the backseat, a slow smile on her face. Katia is sure Evie just had the best orgasm of her life; she is sure every single one of Evie's orgasms is the best of her life.

All four of them are sprawled on the hoods of the cars—boys on one, girls on the other. They listen to the lullaby of the motorway and stare up at the dirty orange sky. The night air smells hot and dense. Beneath a low moon, the town cowers: smokestacks, parking lots, roundabouts. Everything has washed out to gray. Katia and Evie share a cigarette, ringing the filter with sticky lip-gloss in varying shades of pink.

Katia smokes like she's sucking a cock, slow and deliberate, a performance. She knows Evie is watching her, and she arches her body slightly on the hood so Evie can see the curve of her back-hips-tits. Katia knows Evie has a crush on her because she's older and always has a boyfriend. Katia has a crush on Evie too, because she has high round tits and a rosebud mouth and makes amazing noises when she fucks. Evie likes Katia because she is jaded, and Katia likes Evie because she is not.

The boys are still looking up at the sky, but they start to make grumbling noises. They want cigarettes, beer, music. They start jingling the car keys in their pockets, but the road down the hill is pitted and neither car's suspension makes any difference.

Without conferring, the girls slide off the hood, their skirts riding up and flashing their brightly colored thongs. Hand in hand, they walk down the winding hill toward the beacon of the all-night garage.

Wearing sunglasses inside at night makes Evie feel like a movie star. They aren't just a conceit: the fluorescents inside the garage are blinding after the dim glow of the car's interior light. Evie's calves are itching and gray from the dusty path, her skirt stuck to her thighs with sweat. The garage's air-conditioning is cold enough to make her nipples harden, and she crosses her arms over her chest so the guy behind the counter can't see. She paws through the meager collection of wares. Tree-shaped air fresheners, trees on the labels of the mineral water, *Country Life* magazines full of trees. It's fucking stupid: nothing around here even resembles a tree.

Katia snorts, and Evie looks up. Katia is standing, arms akimbo, face raised to the top shelf of the magazine rack. She waits for Evie to walk over then grabs an armful of the magazines. Evie looks over Katia's shoulder at the plastic-wrapped covers showing girls with glazed eyes and black bars over their nipples. She's close enough to smell Katia's hair: sweet fruity shampoo under bitter hairspray. Katia pulls one of the magazines out of the plastic bag and flips through it. Every page is a different girl, her hair dyed and legs spread. There are no black bars on the inside pages, and the girls' cunts are spread open, the bull's-eye of every image.

Evie's clit throbs. The images aren't sexy, but she can't stop staring at the honesty of their open legs. Their tits are clearly fake, high on their ribs and beach ball–tight. But their cunts are pure truth: wet and pink, like steak freshly cut. Evie wonders whether Katia's clit is throbbing too.

Katia is pretty sure she knows more about Evie's sexual tastes from those blurry glimpses through the car window than her own boyfriend. Although Evie is acting like she's totally unfazed by the array of cunts, Katia knows otherwise. She can tell by the way Evie is shifting her weight from one leg to the other, the way she's chewing on her lip, the loudening of her breath. When Evie walked over to the magazine rack, Katia could see her nipples through the thin fabric of her bikini top. Katia knows that Evie can probably see her nipples too, but she doesn't give a shit. She doesn't even care if the perv behind the counter can see. Katia has great tits, and she knows it, and so the whole fucking world can stare.

Katia jams the magazines back onto the top shelf and turns to Evie. She looks stoned, pupils huge and mouth hanging slack. Katia pulls Evie's chin, opening her mouth farther, imagining it will snap back and start rolling up window blind–style like in a cartoon. It's meant to be a joke, but standing there with her heat-swollen hands on Evie's jaw she can see the tiny lines of her lip, can feel the stickiness of her lip-gloss on the tip of her thumb, and it doesn't feel very funny. Katia is suddenly aware of the buzzing fluorescents, the dust itching her legs, the slow stare of the man behind the counter. Her clit feels swollen, her nipples tight. All the pressure in the air seems to coalesce between her legs.

She knows what she should do: let go of Evie, buy cigarettes for the boys, go back out into the dusty night and climb the hill back to that sweaty backseat. She takes Evie's hand and leads her out the back door of the garage.

Walking outside feels like crawling under a blanket. The air is hot and completely still, and Evie can feel the sweat already prickling on the small of her back. She hopes her palms won't feel wet against Katia's. Her whole body feels tight, her skin as thin as an expanding balloon.

They forgot to buy the cigarettes, and Evie is about to mention it when Katia spins her around and presses her up against the brick wall of the garage and slides her tongue into Evie's mouth. All the blood rushes out of Evie's head. She kisses Katia back just to stay standing. The atmosphere is so humid she can barely take a breath, the air like cotton wool in her lungs.

Katia kisses hard, but her lips are soft and she tucks Evie's hair behind her ear before pulling away to smile at her. Evie has Katia's tits pressed up against her tits, Katia's legs tangled in her legs, Katia's fingers entwined with her fingers. All she can think to do is return the smile. Katia seems to take this as consent. She lifts Evie's hair in her hands, piling it up and pressing her palms against the heat of Evie's neck, before kissing her again.

Katia has two heartbeats, one in her chest and one between her legs, and she's pressed up so close to Evie that she must be able to feel both. Evie's skin smells sweet and metallic: fresh perspiration and sugary lip-gloss and boys. Evie's body feels unfamiliar pressed against her own, with bumps where boys don't have them and an absence where they usually do. Katia wonders how she is supposed to know if Evie wants to fuck—she's used to the reassurance of a hard cock against her hip. She stops for a moment, unsure, and Evie wriggles against her, pressing her pelvic bone against Katia's, and then she knows for sure that Evie wants to fuck.

Evie loves having her nipples sucked, and judging from the way Katia immediately takes them into her mouth, she seems aware of the fact. She sucks hard, and Evie's thong is already sliding up into her slickening cunt, the fabric uncomfortable against her swollen clit. Evie's skirt is up around her hips, her bikini top shoved to the side, and she pushes her thong down with one hand and guides Katia's fingers into her with the other.

Katia slides two fingers in, curling them round so the pads press against that little patch of ridged skin, the web between finger and thumb pressing against Evie's clit. Evie can't make words so she just rolls her eyes up to the fading sky and rides Katia's fingers, feeling her wetness pool in Katia's palm. Katia presses her up against the gritty brick wall, fucking her harder, and then Evie feels it, the crest of the wave, the tip of the mountain, and the feeling throbs from her clit to her throat and back down again to settle low in her belly. She can feel her cunt spasming around Katia's fingers, and before the feeling fades she drops to her knees and pulls Katia's thong to the side.

Katia's cunt tastes like wet dirt and salt, and it doesn't matter that Evie doesn't know what she's supposed to do because as soon as she finds that little knot of flesh she hooks on to it, sucking it into her mouth, and Katia is grabbing the back of her head and grinding against her chin and she can feel Katia's cunt spasming against her tongue. The girls stagger to their feet, eyes blurred and knees unsteady. They rearrange their clothes without looking, awkward around each other's nakedness, and walk away from the garage.

As they reach the bottom of the hill, the first drops of a

summer storm land on their shoulders. It's cool against their heat-swollen skin, slicking their hair against their heads; droplets slide down their backs. They raise their faces to the sky. The crackle of heat fades and the smell of earth rises up around them. By the time they get back to their men, the rain has washed them clean.

HUSH

Treasure Sapphire

She is smiling at me from across the room, teeth bared posses-
sively, assured of the power that she has over me. Our eyes are
locked and though there are dozens, maybe even a hundred
women swarming and writhing around us, we can only see each
other.

She brings the long neck of a beer bottle to her lips and
drinks, never breaking her eye contact with me. I press an unlit
cigarette to my lips, an invitation, and in no time she is standing
before me, head cocked charmingly to one side, lighter flickering
in her palm. She ignites me. I thank her.

She is shorter than I am, a solid five six to my lanky five nine
but what she lacks in height she more than makes up for in
cockiness. Her short black hair frames her tanned face perfectly,
and I can tell by the way that she rolls her *r*'s that she is not
American. She asks me my name and I lean forward and whisper
syllables into her ear: "Loretta." She nods and I offer my ear to
her into which she whispers "Lu-ca," spreading the word into

two. I drop my cigarette to the floor and she expertly crushes the cherry beneath the heel of her boot.

She turns to leave and I follow. There are no words exchanged. We slip into a darkened hallway, where she pushes me gently against the wall. I let her hold me there, relinquishing my power for just a moment. Her hand snakes around me, pulling me closer, and I know that she can feel it pressing into her. Her gasp is tinged with confusion and arousal.

Suddenly a thick band of white light envelops us; two giggling women walk past and we duck into the restroom they've just left. I can see her clearly now. See him. Luca. He is wearing a tight black shirt, breasts undoubtedly bound beneath it, a pair of tight black jeans and combat boots. His body is muscular and rolling, even golden color all over.

I step back to let him see me: the skintight red dress, the matching red lipstick and the hair that cascades down my back. He lunges at me, lips against mine, pressing my bare back onto the cold tiles of the bathroom wall. He grinds his hips into me as he expertly lowers the top of my dress, freeing my breasts. I can feel the warmth of his tongue and then the heat of his breath playing over my swollen nipples. I wrap my hand around his head and hold him there. His other hand sneaks up my smooth thigh, pushing my dress aside, and I can hear his hoarse breathing as he pulls down my panties. He is staring at the delicate straps that hug my hips, his fingers curled around the tip of my length.

I look into the mirror and see myself half naked, pressed into the wall with Luca staring down at my cock, and my clit begins to throb. Before I even have to ask him he has dropped to his knees and taken me into his mouth. I watch as his thin lips caress me, then as his tongue flickers softly across the head of my cock before hungrily taking me all the way into the back of his throat. The force of his bobbing head thrusts the cock back into me repeatedly, rubbing maddeningly over my swollen clit.

I lift him up off the ground and twirl him around until he is now in my former position, back against the wall. I instruct him to watch me in the mirror. I kiss the side of his neck, tracing against his jawline with my tongue, letting my hand slide down his flat, muscular stomach until it arrives just beneath his jeans but staying above his jockeys.

I dip my hand into the apex between his legs and feel the scorching wetness there, and when I apply pressure he moans. I drop to my knees, unbuckling his belt and pushing his pants down to his ankles. I slide my fingers along the band of his underwear, pressing my lips to the flesh just below his belly button before curling my fingers around them and pulling them down and off along with his pants. I look up at his face riddled with arousal and remind him to watch me in the mirror.

I take his leg and latch it over my shoulder before burying my face between his thighs. The second my tongue touches him, his breathing deepens, becomes harder, faster. I swirl my tongue up and down the cleft, flicking her clit with my tongue and becoming more and more excited every time I hear him groan. His hands are on my shoulders, fingernails dug in, and the slight pain spurs me to lick faster, harder. He wants release and I yearn to give it to him but not like this.

I stand and look into his eyes before drawing him into a kiss and spinning his body around again. We are looking at ourselves in the mirror above the sink. I run my hand up his back and apply the slightest bit of pressure until he gets the hint and leans forward, bent at the hips. I reach down and slide my finger into his wetness before wrapping a firm hand around my cock and guiding it into him.

She gasps and trembles as I spread her open, working my way slowly inside, watching his face as every inch sinks in. I go easy at first, awestruck by the look of pure ecstasy on Luca's face: The beauty of it. The handsomeness of it. He lets out a low growl (or perhaps I do), and suddenly I cannot control myself. I am thrusting so hard that the mirror above the sink begins to shake ominously, causing our reflections to distort and blur.

I look down and watch myself pushing in and out of him, my cock covered with his cum.

The friction against my clit is relentless. I reach around to play my fingers over her, jacking him off while I continue thrusting shamelessly in and out. His body tightens and his hands, knuckles white from the tension of gripping on to the sides of the sink, tremble underneath the weight of our pistoning bodies. Suddenly he wails, body jerking and convulsing beneath mine. I give one final thrust and my clit explodes. I grab on to him tightly, fingers still buried between his thighs.

It takes us a moment to recover. I fix my dress and tuck my panties into my purse while he pulls his pants and briefs back on. Once dressed, we stare at each other wordlessly. I fumble through my purse and then press a cigarette to my lips. Without even having to be asked I hand her one as well. She flicks her lighter, holding the flame out to me. I puff the thin stick gingerly. We smile, and then we both exit the restroom.

BLOOD LUST

Giselle Renarde

I have no specific recollection of how Cat came into my life. One day she was just there, lying on my bed. She seemed to know me, I seemed to know her, and after one of the longest dry spells known to dykedom, that was good enough.

"Come to bed," she purred. She always seemed to be purring. Maybe that's why she was called *Cat*. I couldn't remember if it was a nickname or a diminutive of Cathleen or Catalina. At that point I was too embarrassed to ask. I was supposed to know her. The way she talked, it seemed like she'd been in my bed for ages, and I was only just waking up to her.

"Look at the time," Cat said. She drew open the bedsheets, inviting me in. Had I ever seen her in that cotton cami or those little ruffled boy shorts? Everything about her—even her clothes—seemed hazily familiar, like I knew them from a dream. "Come on," she begged, with a pretty pout on her pink lips. "It's late."

"Late? It's only two." I felt like she ought to know I didn't consider two in the morning *late*, but at the same time I didn't really know *what* she knew. "I work better at night," I explained, but that didn't seem relevant to her.

"You shouldn't stay up sketching all night," she teased. Her voice had the warmth of a cashmere blanket. When she spoke, I wanted to wrap myself in her words. "Do you want to turn into a vampire or something?"

The innocence of her tone made me chuckle. "Yup, that's it," I said. "All artists want to be vampires. That's why we work under the cover of darkness."

"Oh." She stretched out like a tabby. The way she looked at me, with total honesty, made me wonder if she didn't take me a little too seriously. But when she raised her eyebrows and crossed her long legs like a pinup model, work was the last thing on my mind.

Setting down my pencil, I crawled on top of her and nuzzled in. Somehow I knew she'd giggle. As I kissed up and down her neck, she laughed so loudly I'm sure my neighbors thought they were in on our joke. "Suck my neck," she cried, loudly. Her lithe body writhed beneath me. "Bite me!"

I wrapped my lips over my teeth like a toothless granny and chomped on her neck. She giggled so hard I thought she was going to die. I loved that something so simple evoked such a huge reaction. "Stop, stop," she wheezed between sputters of laughter. "Stop, I can't breathe!"

Showing mercy, I leaned away for a second. Her chest heaved as she sighed, giggled, sighed, giggled, her pixie face framed with messy orange curls. The weathered cotton of her cami was so sheer I could see her pink nipples forming tight buds underneath as her breathing regulated. A surge of electricity shot through me. I barely knew who she was, but I knew I couldn't resist her.

Pulling her top off, I dove at her white little tits and sucked her hard nipples. They were like candy on my tongue. I loved her tits. If I had two heads, I'd have sucked them both at once. She ran her hands through my hair, moving my mouth from breast to breast as I thrust my hand beneath her shorts. Her slit was wet and waiting. When my fingers dove inside, she sighed and grasped my hair in her little fists. If I sucked hard, I could get her whole tit in my mouth, but she seemed more interested in the finger-fucking.

"I want to take this to the next level," she panted. In my books that meant fisting, but as I prepared to give her another finger she let go of my hair and rolled onto her belly.

I gasped as she fished through my night table. "Your back!" Why did her back come as such a shock when her clothes and her lips and her hair seemed so familiar? Had I never seen it before? Had she never rolled over naked in my bed?

Looking up at me, her eyes wide with alarm, she asked, "What's wrong?"

My head seemed to be shaking of its own volition. My whole body felt prickly and hot. I was horrified. Or was I fascinated? Maybe both. I was transfixed, at any rate. Her back was carved up like...well, really, the only comparison I could draw was, "You've got a back like a bathroom wall!"

A cheeky grin bled across her lips. "I like that," she said. "*A back like a bathroom wall*. I've never thought of it that way."

"Who did this to you?" I asked, though it was obviously more than one person. There were different names, phone numbers, quotes and political messages, styles of handwriting. Was it still considered *writing* when it was carved into a girl's back?

"Some people get tattoos every time they think they're in love," Cat reasoned. Her tone was dreamy and casual. She turned her head until her chin rested on her left shoulder, and pointed to the name there. "The first girl I slept with was Roxanne. I thought I was in love with her."

All I could do was stare. I didn't want to touch it—I didn't want to hurt her—but I wanted to know how her scars would feel against my skin. "And this was her idea of a tattoo?" I asked, tracing the big *x* in the name with my fingertip.

"No, that was her idea of *love*," Cat replied. She shuddered as I stroked it. Her scar was the softest skin I'd ever touched. "Love and possession were the same thing to Roxanne. She sat on my back. She wasn't big, but she had some serious muscle to her. She sat with her ass in the curve of my back and her knees pressing my arms into her carpet, and she pulled this knife out of her pocket."

Fishing around in the drawer of my night table, she finally found what she was looking for: a scalpel with a shiny metal grip. When she passed the knife to me, I was surprised by its weight in my hand. "She took her time marking me with it. She dragged the knife into my skin and I could feel it cutting through me. Just one straight line to start the *R*. I could feel that I was bleeding, but she leaned down and drank up every drop. No good wasting it on the carpet, she said. She did another line and drank the blood from that one, but then she said that was enough for one night..."

"For one night?" I stammered, shaking my head. I wouldn't have believed it if I hadn't had my finger on the very *R* she was talking about.

"Yes," Cat replied with a simple nod. "And I promised to stay with her until she'd finished putting her name in my skin. We did a little more each time. She'd lick my pussy or fuck me with her fingers, and then as the grand finale, she'd carve me up. We never lost a drop of blood to the carpet."

"What?" I didn't want to seem judgmental, but it was just crazy, wasn't it?

Handing me the scalpel, Cat giggled, "The bathroom wall wasn't built in a day. It's taken years to get to this point."

With a combination of nausea and awe, I traced my finger down from *Roxanne*, through a phone number with an international area code, and the words *Art is Life*. There were more names than I could stand to read. Though I felt no sense of ownership over Cat, it hurt me to think of her with all those other people. I wouldn't let myself count how many names had stained her back with blood. But the worst part was that mine wasn't one of them. Looking down at the scalpel I thought, *The next person to hold this thing will never know I was here.* I had to leave my mark.

Cat rested her head on my pillow. She wasn't looking at me when she asked, "Do you want to add your name to the *bathroom wall?*"

"Yes," I replied before she'd finished speaking.

The biggest space I could find was down in her lower back, nearly along her side. Anywhere else, I'd have to condense my name to a diminutive, but I felt like if I was going ahead with this I might as well carve *Marjane* out in full.

My heart raced as I visualized the knife cutting the first line of the *M*. I traced the scalpel through the air, imagining exactly what that line would look like: mostly straight, with a slight curve at the bottom.

"Remember to catch my blood after you make the cut," Cat called as I leaned in to put scalpel to skin. "Best way is with your tongue. Just suck it up. It'll heal faster, too."

"Okay," I agreed, leaning in very close. I rested the point of the scalpel millimetres away from her flesh and held that position so long my hand started to cramp. What was I waiting for? Pressing the tip of the knife into her skin, I drew it down, around and out in one swift motion.

Cat shrieked in what sounded like half pain and half orgasm. I licked the line of blood tumbling down her flesh. The moment that thick metallic redness met my tongue, I knew I could never go back. Those few drops of sweet blood seemed to course through my veins, warming my toes and exploding like a supernova in my pussy. I gasped at the sensation her life force generated in me.

Setting the scalpel on my night table, I flipped her onto her side and grabbed at her tits as I licked the incision. I felt like an animal. Her blood made me wild. As I sucked the blood, my throbbing clit drove me to trib on anything close by—and that *anything* ended up being her smoothly-shaven leg. I suckled her side. She nourished me. Her blood ran hot through my body, and I knew if I didn't get to feel her wet pussy on mine I would lose my mind.

In one motion, I tore off Cat's ruffled boy shorts and pressed them against the bleeding line in her side. Her legs were long but her body easy to manipulate. When I tucked my body neatly between her legs, she sighed, "Oh, Mari, Mari, Mari," and my lungs just about exploded. Her voice contained all the passion of the willingly seduced.

Cat threw her leg over my shoulder. I kissed it, leaving a path of red blood as I sunk into the V of her thighs. She pressed her wet pussy against mine, and I pressed back against her moist folds. Together, we were *juice*. We were one big pool of pussy juice lapping like waves against distant shores. The pressure of her wet lips on mine drove me wild. My body burned with her blood.

Neighbors be damned. I cried out in an ecstasy of blood and sweat as my soul blazed. Cat was shouting too, incomprehensible niceties as she circled her hips to press against me. We were stuck, pussy to pussy, bound together in a writhing mass that seemed more than the two we were. As I lay face up on my bed with a strange girl between my legs, I felt a sense of invigoration attached to my postcoital exhaustion.

"I can't believe I licked your blood," I said, in amazement. It occurred to me I should clean her wound with something more than my tongue, but when I lifted her little cotton shorts from her side there was nothing there but a clean cut in her flesh. No blood. I stared in disbelief. "I cut you. You bled. Why aren't you bleeding now?"

Cuddling her head on my pillow, she giggled. "I told you your tongue would seal it up." Her eyes seemed to melt from sky blue to sea-foam green as she held my gaze. "How did it taste?"

"Good," I said. I could still taste the metallic sweetness of her blood on my lips. When I licked them, all her strength surged through me. "It tastes incredible, actually." So incredible I began to crave not only its taste but also the surge of fiery power that coursed through my body with every lick. Each night I carved a new line and sucked the blood from her fresh wound. She gave herself over to me. When I looked at her back, I didn't see a bathroom wall anymore. I saw generosity of spirit. Cat was the most benevolent creature I'd ever known.

It would take twenty-three nights, I estimated, to spell out MARJANE all in capital letters.

"What are you?" I asked on that final evening. Only the last line of my *E* remained to be carved. As I sketched her, I could only think how *normal* she looked. She couldn't be human, could she? Was I? At one time yes, but not anymore. I could feel the change in my body and my cravings.

"I told you when we met," she said with a smile. "I told you who I am."

My pencil scratched against the paper as I shaded her inner thighs. That night, she wore a satin slip that barely covered her hips when she lay on her side. I licked my lips. Sex and blood were becoming one in my mind. Cat had everything I wanted. "I don't remember," I confessed. I hoped she wouldn't be upset.

With a chuckle, she said, "I'm the Catalyst. You wanted to switch your days to nights. You wanted to give your life over to art. I am *the way*. I'm the means to that end."

I didn't understand, and that's what I told her, though I suspected if I'd concentrated more on the conversation and less on my art I might have figured it out on my own. As much as I wanted to put down my pencil, I couldn't do it until I'd finished her portrait. It was the only way for me to keep her, in any sense.

"Haven't you ever heard that art is life?" she giggled. I couldn't get over how coy she was, even though she was living in my bed.

"Sure," I said, still putting pencil to paper. "It's carved into your back—*Art is Life*."

"You want to be a true artist," she replied, tracing her big toe up the back of the opposite calf. "Where do you suppose all that life force comes from? If it came from you, your art would eat you alive. You'd be dead in a day. If you want to create like the masters, you have to live like them." Taking the scalpel from my night table, she held it up like an instrument of worship. "I've given you a taste. Now you have the blood lust. I've been your mother and suckled you with my life, but after tonight you'll be on your own to procure your meals. Do you think you can handle that?"

My pencil fell from my hand. "No," I said. My head seemed to be shaking. I couldn't stop it, even as I dropped my sketch and ran to join her on my bed. "You're my source, Cat. If you leave me, I'll die of thirst."

She ran her fingers through my hair and planted a sweet kiss on my forehead. "You can fly, baby bird," she assured me. "I know you'll figure it out."

"No, I really won't." I was starting to panic, but her smile reassured me.

"Where's your confidence gone?" she asked. "You're more innovative than you know, so don't go asking me where your next meal is coming from. I can only tell you where to get your *last supper*." She cocked her eyebrow as she handed me the scalpel. "Finish the *E*."

The instrument had never felt so heavy in my hand. I suppose I must have known all along my ginger Cat was initiating me into another realm of existence, but I hadn't counted on her leaving until I was ready to let her go. Now the end was drawing near.

She sighed into my pillow as I traced the knife through her flesh. The sensation of cutting deep into her skin was familiar to me now, but no less invigorating. After a brief moment of molecular shock, small drops of red rose to the surface. My legs quivered even though I was sitting. My heart seemed to beat in double time. I licked my lips.

Tossing the scalpel to the night table, I threw my face at her side and savored the taste. Her blood ran through me as I sucked it from her body. Its sweetness filled my cheeks and its warmth burned inside me. She sighed at the sensation, but I knew how nice she'd feel if I pressed my palm against her pussy.

Cat seized up, tossing her head back on my pillow. As I squeezed her pussy lips together, she moaned my name, *Marjane*, and pressed her thighs tight around my hand. I stroked her gorgeous slit. Her juice soaked my bare fingers while her blood drenched my lips. When she reached under my top and grabbed my tits, I sucked her side with renewed vigor. Her soft hands felt incredible. *Why does she have to leave?* She squeezed my breasts as I lapped her blood in ecstasy. *Why can't she stay with me? Nourish me? Feed me?*

My hand went wild on her slippery clit and she threw her head to the side, pinching my nipple hard. Her sweet blood coated my lips when she came loud as ever. She was pain and she was joy. Her scream was the cry of an infant entering this world with the wisdom of the ages. She gave me all.

How can I describe Cat but to say she was my creator and my creation? She was the Catalyst who sparked my blood lust. She was my artist's enabler. Without her, what would I be? *Normal?* What artist could live that way? *Normality, mediocrity*—artists cringe at these words.

I don't remember Cat leaving. Of course, I didn't remember her coming either. In and out like a lamb, but a lion in the interim. I understood why she had to leave. There were others like me, other artists fated to add their names to her bathroom wall. She had to tend to them all, and there was only one of her. In that sense, I marvel at the number of weeks she devoted to my personal catalysis. The taste of her sweet blood planted a longing in my veins, but I'm on my own now, fending for myself. It's a task in everyday eroticism and as sexually charged as you can imagine, but not as challenging as I'd anticipated. You'd be surprised how many backs are out there, just waiting to be scratched.

THE PRODUCE QUEEN

Michelle Brennan

I have a confession to make, a dirty little secret, a skeleton to pull out of the closet. I like produce. Rather, I love produce—in fact, I might even be in love with the endless array of fresh fruits and vegetables that satiate my excitable palate every day. It's not something I can comfortably talk about with my friends just yet. While the girls sit around the office fawning over their latest Perez Hilton–approved celebrity crush, there just doesn't seem to be any appropriate place to put in a good word for the solid and committed cucumber I enjoyed the night before.

My heightened appreciation for fruitage began innocently enough when a lover slipped a condom-covered Clementine up my cunt and instructed me not to drop it. I swooned with sweet delight at the challenge. My clit was tortured and teased mercilessly, with taunts of what would happen were I to lose it; however, my Kegel muscles are well trained, thanks to Betty Dodson, and I managed to keep that little bulb tight in its instructed spot.

Soon after my date with Clementine Cutie Pie, I began to notice that my commute home from work was taking longer than usual. Before I realized what I was doing, I found myself at the farm stand by my office, gazing wistfully at the grapefruits and giving them a little squeeze to see how ripe they were. I'd move on to the peaches and my eyes would gleam while I tickled their fuzz, hypnotized by their intoxicating perfume, then I'd snag a few blueberries to pop in my mouth before racing home to make dinner.

My obsession with food only got worse as the weeks passed, and I could barely make a salad without some ingredient tempting me to play dirty games. On one sunny spring afternoon, I was traipsing through the farm stand when I came upon the loveliest avocado I'd ever laid eyes upon. Its ripeness was pure perfection, giving in ever so gently between my squeezing fingers. Inside that rough outer exterior was a supple, creamy, bright green center, and I could taste its guacamole. Warmth crept between my thighs as I scurried up to the cashier. There were only two people in front of me, but their sizable purchases made my foot start to tap uncontrollably, although it wasn't their fault that I was eager to embark on a date with the most supreme avocado in the market.

On the way home, I was like a high school girl on a first date. I could wait no longer! I stopped at a dark and deserted passage covered with old graffiti tags and broken beer bottles, a safe haven for any alley dweller. On this particular day, the dwellers were dwelling elsewhere, and I wasn't focused on anything other than what was in my brown bag, so I took a swift turn between the two tall buildings and gave my sweet avocado a little shake in its bag.

The darkness blanketed us in solitude, and I felt wet and warm between my thighs as I hid behind some Dumpsters. I bunched up my skirt and began to touch myself, playing with my clit, rubbing my sweet nectar all over my cunt, teasing myself until I could resist no more. I pulled that bright green avocado out of the brown bag it was dressed in and gave it a little shower with my bottled water. Ooh, it glimmered and gleamed, even in the shadows, and I tried to silence my own delicious squeal as I felt the small end of my sweet temptation slip right into my soaking, self-lubricated cunt. I held on to its base and let the chilly brick wall catch me as I leaned back and fucked myself. It just felt so…so…liberating to be in this alley, just me and my avo; its rough, ridged rind grinding against my G-spot when I positioned it just right, feeling my muscles squeezing, yearning to take it all in. I reached down with my free hand and circled around my clit, starting out gently and quickly adding more pressure as she grew more sensitive. Goose bumps crept up my arms, and sweat began to bead along my hairline. I could feel pressure building down between my hips, and I found a steady rhythm to ride that little pleasurable treat into a flood of orgasmic relief, weeks of tension and anticipation spilling past my produce and down the inside of my thighs.

One orgasm was good, but two would be better! I worked up the excitement in my cunt once more, thinking about that Clementine Cutie again. I could almost feel those soft hands, that menacing growl issuing explicit instructions to keep the citrus in place. The rush of heat to my ears warmed my entire body and I turned as red as the bricks holding me up. Before I knew it, nearly the whole avocado disappeared into my cunt. I dared not let go of its base, as I would not have any assistance in retrieving it were it to move past my pelvic bone. It was so good and filling, but I wanted to feel stuffed by my new toy. I withdrew the avocado, turned it around, then worked the wider base of the fruit back into my cunt. Oh, my! This side was firmer and hadn't been warmed up yet by my cunt walls, making it a surprising and delightful addition to my pleasure. I loved the sensation of being so full, but the pressure of my cunt squeezing was starting to soften the avocado a bit. I couldn't breathe fast enough. I pushed it in and out, moving quickly, working up small moans that echoed against the buildings. The terror of getting caught rode through my brain, and it made my cunt swell with anticipation and excitement. I could feel my cunt making that sweet, creamy inside softer. I was in love with this avocado, as I crept over the edge to erupt with an orgasm that far surpassed the first one, and I could feel sweet honey cum dripping down the inside of my legs.

My bottom lip hurt, and I realized I had been biting down on it, trying to keep quiet. My breaths slowed as I slowly released the avocado from between my legs, rinsed it off again, and sighed. I took a swig of water, regained my balance and ran to catch the bus.

It had definitely been the best appetizer I'd ever enjoyed, and I looked forward to a delicious dinner later that night.

HOT YOGA

Anne Grip

The buzz in her pocket sent Natalie's hopes sky high. *Please be Dex*, she thought—the same wish she made any time a text came through.

1:17PM Dex: wanna come 2 yoga 2nite???

Ugh. No way. Dex was always going on about her awesome queer yoga class and how much energy it gave her and how great the community was and blah blah blah. Yoga? On a Friday night? She rolled her eyes, thinking of the wholesome types that would be there and how her scrawny programmer ass would not fit in. She had to put a stop to this.

1:19PM Natalie: fuck downward dog! i wanna do the new queer sex party!!!

1:20PM Dex: cmon-yoga 1st! i told u my teacher=sex on a mat.

1:22PM Natalie: uhhhh. u kno yoga is cringe 4 me.

1:23PM Dex: veggie burgers on me after? then we hit party, k?

Natalie set the phone down and ran her hands through the fine dark hair that flopped over her face, the curtain she kept between herself and the world, so she could avoid eye contact. She had been on edge for weeks, ever since Dex mentioned that Consummate, a pansexual sex party for queers, was starting up at a sex club in Hell's Kitchen. And unlike the first sex party that Dex had taken her to, this one required that participants wear only underwear.

Her phone skittered across the desk with a loud buzz.

1:31PM Dex: k???

There was only one thing that could drag her ass to yoga. She looked at the icon of Dex mugging for the camera and smiled.

1:32PM Natalie: k. c u there ;)

Shit! Now she *had* to go to yoga. Dex was like a magnet that drew her out into the world. Nat had crushed on her the instant they met at the Linux User Group in November: another brown queer geek in a room full of cis boy nerds. She loved their late-night Skypes deconstructing the various incarnations of "Doctor Who" or the uselessness of identity politics in growing up biracial, but what kept her up even later was the thought of sliding her hands under Dex's sweater vest to touch the warm flesh underneath. She was just never sure how mutual it was. Mutual enough to make out twice now, yeah, okay, but she knew Dex went out and had casual hookups from sex parties and off Craigslist. But not with her. Not yet. That could either be good or bad, but, she hoped, not indifferent.

Dex adjusted her oversized glasses. "So, what did you think of class?"

Natalie finished off a French fry. "Not bad. I didn't feel totally humiliated."

"Let me be more specific, what did you think of the carbon-based life forms you shared the class with. Lets start with our fearless leader, Edgar."

"Okay, he's ridiculously hot. Why didn't you tell me?" Natalie had stored many mental images from the ninety-minute class. His broad cheekbones made him look serene; his curly hair, boyish. Natalie had found it hard to hear his instructions, distracted by his immaculately shaped lips. Even as she had admired his T-shirt stretching across his pectorals, she wondered what he would look like without it, or the disappointingly roomy shorts he wore.

"I think actually I have told you that for the past three months," Dex reminded her.

"So, you're right. How do you concentrate anyway, with him standing there, looking all radiant?"

Dex sipped her spirulina smoothie. "I find it helps my practice. He seems to regulate my breathing simply by being a specimen of symmetry and balance. Did he give you any assists?"

"Just the one doing triangle pose." Natalie had felt him come up behind her and mutely nodded yes when he asked, "May I?" His left hand rolled her left hip backward while his right hand kept a constant pressure on her right hip. The slight shift seemed to make energy shoot out of her raised hand—and set off the sensation of a low frequency buzz in her groin. "Good," he murmured as she held it. She felt sad when he moved on to help the person in front of her, wishing she could give him other things to fix.

"Yeah," Dex agreed, deadpan as ever, "he's totally perfected my *trikonasana*. Some hot queers show up though, huh? Did you see the cute girl in the front row? All pierced up with the short, spiky hair?"

Natalie scrunched her forehead. She had noticed precisely one girl in class: Dex. Even facing forward, she had felt Dex's presence, like a magnet that never left her with any doubt as to which direction she wanted to turn.

"You are hopeless sometimes," Dex said with a laugh. "Okay, let's try again. Did you notice that other guy? Bearded? Kind of like a baby bear?"

"Oh, yeah! He was *totally* adorable."

"I figured you would notice the boys. *That* would be Edgar's boyfriend," Dex announced.

"The two of them? Oh, that's so hot." They both sat for a moment and slurped the froth at the bottom of their drinks in silent agreement.

"Well, you should have plenty of guys to perv on tonight. This party space is supposed to be amazing: slings, glory holes, showers, the works! Or you can just watch the porn and pretend you're home."

Natalie felt her face burn. "So...I like to watch."

"Oh, I know," Dex smiled. She pushed back from the table and flexed her arms over her head. "Now that we're all warmed up, lets head into the city."

Natalie handed over her cash to the coat check stud, who wore a pair of black boxer briefs as casually as if he were fully dressed. She tried not to gawk at his chiseled abs and wondered why it felt hard to pay the thirty-dollar cover. He gave her a friendly wink. "It's an underwear party, although you are, of course, encouraged to be naked. You can strip down in that room right there. Here's your key for the locker."

"Thanks." She bent over to reach for her bag, then froze as she realized what was missing. "Oh, fuck. Dex! My other bag—I must have left it at the restaurant!"

"Oh, that sucks."

Dex parted the curtain and went into the locker room. Natalie followed her in.

"No. You don't understand. My underwear was in that bag."

"You're not wearing underwear?"

"My *party* underwear," Natalie emphasized.

"Just wear your cutoff yoga sweats. They're sort of under-weary. But sketchy. Very American Apparel for flashers."

Natalie grimaced, unconvinced. "I had these cute new Puma boxer briefs."

"And they're back in Brooklyn, so it doesn't matter. Just go with it," Dex said.

Natalie stripped hurriedly, wanting to cover up as quickly as possible before anyone else joined them. Bottomless, she slid into her shorts and switched from her T-shirt into a gray A-shirt. She shoved her street clothes in her tiny locker and looked in the full-length mirror. With her Converse sneakers and her jock-y looking outfit, she did look kind of sketchy. Going commando added to her disreputable feeling. She liked the way her shoulders looked: Scrappy. Ready for anything. She looked like someone who was going to be able to walk out of this room and into a party of mostly naked strangers in New York City. Yeah. Totally. She could totally do this. Because there was no reason to panic. Absolutely none. She caught the look in her eyes, hiding behind shaggy bangs. Hopefully nobody would be able to notice her freaking out.

"You like?"

Natalie turned around to see Dex topless in a pair of vivid yellow briefs with purple piping. She stared at the huge bulge jutting sideways from her crotch. Uh, yeah, she liked.

"I had to buy a size large to make room for this," Dex propped her hand on the obscene package as she checked herself out in the mirror. "I thought it would be welcoming, you know, in a subtle way."

"*Subtle?*"

Dex turned to Natalie, grabbed her hand and cupped it

on the bulge distending her underwear. "Yeah," Dex's mouth came close to one ear. "Sometimes you just want to get to know someone better."

Natalie felt something pulsing like a drum, probably not the hard sex toy her hand had involuntarily squeezed. Dex's words, or her breath on Natalie's neck, had hardened her nipples. Nat swallowed and ran her tongue across her dry lips. "Um, I don't think we should do this in here."

"In the changing room of a sex club? Yeah, we should probably tone it down, you're right," Dex agreed. Dex pulled on a mesh tank top, dark purple to match the trim on her underwear and her purple-and-yellow high-top Nikes. With one last glance at her reflection she smoothed her carefully shaped Afro and grabbed Natalie's hand. "Let's go."

Dex led them down a hallway toward the rear of the building. Natalie felt her sweat between their mingled hands. They passed a few bodies wandering in the corridors but it was early and no action had started yet. They passed an open cubicle with an empty bed. Dex paused for a moment, considering, but continued on.

"How about here?" Dex asked, stopping them both and backing Natalie into a corner. A tremor passed through Natalie's body. By the glow of a bare red lightbulb from the corridor behind them, Natalie could see Dex in silhouette, standing close but not touching her. Dex returned her hand to her crotch and rubbed it slowly. "Now don't freak out if I get a little hard," she teased.

Nat giggled, then stopped short. Dex had leaned her body forward and Nat felt the oversized hard-on pressing into her pubic bone. She started giggling again as she thought, *Definitely subtle.* A hand brushed the side of her face in a caress. Nat closed her eyes. *Yes, please,* she wanted to say, had she been able to talk. The sensations of hardness down below, warm breath near her throat and the first touch of Dex's lips immobilized her.

She wedged her arms into the rough brick walls on either side, thankful for their solidity. The softness of Dex's kisses as they traversed her skin made her feel like she was evaporating. She opened her mouth, expectant, eager. Dex ran her tongue along Nat's lower lip and ended with a small, sharp bite that jolted Nat's cunt open. Nat grabbed Dex's shoulder and dug in her fingers.

They made out, alternately teasing and grinding as Natalie followed Dex's lead. The music had jumped in volume and people in various states of undress started to flow past them. They stayed put, body to body in the corner, feasting on each other's mouth and skin, letting flesh test weight, muscle tension and release.

Fingers squeezed her nipple and Natalie opened her eyes with a gasp. A cry rang in her ears. Had that been her? She felt all woozy and blurred. It was hard to tell what was inside and what was outside just now. She blinked slowly.

Nat felt a coolness around her body that was new. She opened her eyes and saw that Dex had moved to her side, also leaning against the wall.

"What's up?"

Dex cocked her head. "Let's go see what all those noises are."

Nat couldn't remember hearing anything above the drum of her pounding heart and the bass of the loud club music some-where above them but the moment Dex said that, the sounds from the room beyond them registered. There was a loud smack, a louder scream, then a girl's high-pitched voice: "Thank you, Headmistress!"

"That does sound interesting."

"*Mmm-hmm.* Shall we?" Dex gestured gallantly.

Natalie headed down the hall and stepped into the back room. There were two participants in the middle and the walls around them were lined with watchers.

A woman in a shiny black corset and boots up to her thighs traced her fingers across the reddened bottom of a girl bent over a padded bench. "I can't believe the PE teacher caught you masturbating in the showers *again,* you little slut. I thought after the fifth time I punished you for this that you would learn. But *noooooooooo!*"

"I'm sorry, Headmistress!" *Smack smack smack* rang out, followed by more high-pitched wails from the girl.

Dex whispered, "Remember her? From yoga?"

She did look sort of familiar, although from this direction her main identifying features were the backs of her long legs and the curve of her ass.

The Headmistress picked up a long stick and started whipping it through the air, making a sharp swish with every stroke. "Nobody has ever failed PE at my distinguished learning establishment before. This is an utter disgrace and you are a shameless little whore." The whistling noise of the switch was followed by a piercing cry as it struck flesh.

Natalie touched her own ass, hearing the scream, thinking how much it must have hurt. She snuck a look at Dex, who was absorbed in the scene, a pucker to her mouth that meant she was amused.

The Headmistress put a hand on her hip and let out an exaggerated sigh. "That will be enough of your fussing, young lady." She peeled off the girl's polka-dotted panties and promptly stuffed them in the girl's mouth. The onlookers erupted in laughter.

Seizing the break in the action, Dex pulled her across the room and they watched from the opposite perspective. Natalie could see the concentration in the Domme's face with every throw of the whip. The girl's screams were muted now with the underwear gag in place but she still made full-throated noises as every blow landed. After one strike and the painful response, Natalie was surprised to see that despite all her ado, the girl was grinning, almost laughing.

"She's eating it up, huh?" Dex said, laughing. The volume in the room had risen and there were conversations on either side of them. "Whoa!" Dex said, grabbing her arm, "guess yoga got *everyone* hot and bothered tonight."

Natalie followed her gaze and saw Edgar scoping out the room. He didn't look any different than he had in class except that he was bare-chested and wearing a snug-fitting pair of white briefs. Seeing his perfection on display, Natalie wanted to laugh. If only all fantasies materialized so quickly. Apparently not finding what he was looking for, he left the room.

Dex grabbed Natalie's hand and they followed him out. Dex led her into the maze. There were partitions, with strategic openings at eye and waist level every few feet. They passed by lookers with their faces pressed close to the walls and by open holes that Dex and Nat also looked into, searching for their quarry. They made sure to share any hot sights with each other, bodies huddled close in the narrow space. They passed by scene after scene in the little nooks. Fucking, *check*. Sucking, *check*. Fisting, *check*. Spanking, *check*. But no Edgar.

Dex looked through another peephole and grabbed Nat's arm. "What?" She moved aside and Natalie peered through the hole. Edgar and his hot bear boyfriend, wearing only a jock, were making out. They stood in an open area, alone for the moment, under a bright yellow light. The bear's back was covered in dark curly hair. Edgar's hands gripped his bare bottom, also furry, kneading his buttcheeks. His arms circled his lover, with one hand on Edgar's parabolically curved ass and the other groping his cock through his white underwear.

She thought about relinquishing the view but she felt possessive. They were so beautiful, so unimaginably hot that her breath fought to get around a lump in her throat. She felt a throbbing centered in her groin and pulsing up her gut, almost painful as it built upward.

And then her breath stopped altogether. The bear crouched to his knees and took his boyfriend's cock out of his underwear. She felt her mouth go dry. He stroked the cock slowly, looking up. Edgar rested his hand on his boyfriend's head. She felt the camera in her head take a snapshot. *That's what true love looks like,* she told herself.

Baby Bear (as Nat had taken to thinking of him) removed a condom stashed in his sock and rolled it onto Edgar's engorged prick. He paused for a moment with his hand circling the shaft, his head tilted to the side, lips slightly open. Natalie felt herself start to rock back and forth. She wanted it so bad. As he took the cock in his mouth she exhaled with a groan, as if it were her cock that was being serviced.

"Oh, *yeah*!" she heard Dex rasp, and looked down to her right where Dex had found another glory hole that she was crouching to see through. She grinned, happy to see that Dex was also watching the show, but snapped her attention back to the blow job. This was so much better than porn. It was real. She was so riveted by the sight she didn't want to blink her eyes. Her body synched up with the rhythm of Baby Bear's head, rocking back and forth in time as he took the cock even deeper into his mouth.

"That's it, keep watching, I know you're not going to share that view. Go ahead, keep looking. Watch him getting sucked off." Dex's body pressed against Nat from behind; Dex's mouth was at Nat's ear and a hand slid between her legs and put firm pressure right on her clit.

Natalie felt trapped in the proverbial looking glass. The cocksucking scene had drawn a crowd. She saw that some of the voyeurs lining the walls were stroking their dicks as well, some with full erections. Edgar stood in the middle, an angel in ecstasy as he flexed his body, arching his back, his lips open. Dex kept her pressed flush against the wall, giving her no choice but to watch. She had been turned on before, but now she felt like she was on some kind of drug; a drug that put all the feeling in her cunt while everything else went numb.

Dex moved her body away and started squeezing Nat's ass, first one side then the other. Nat pushed away from the wall, bending back into the sensation, yielding to the hands that worked her with firm intent. She felt like she had been opened up and her cunt throbbed, waiting. Everywhere Dex touched her made her whimper.

"You're really hot when you let go, Nat."

Let go? She was gone. Dex's hand slid in between her legs and grabbed the tender part of her inner thigh. This time her moan was long and low. Her urgency made Dex work faster, yanking her shorts down to the floor in two quick jerks.

"You remember what I brought?"

"Yeah." She felt the fat head of Dex's torpedo cock brush down the cleft of her ass and press forward against her cunt lips. Hands braced against the wall, she looked up and saw the orgy of cocksucking in the next room as the spectators were no longer content to just watch the two men joined in the middle; hands, mouths and pricks were combined in every direction.

A large wet protuberance began to push inside her as Dex's slippery hand grasped her hip for leverage. She spread her feet wider and pushed back to meet the penetration.

Dex was in charge. She wouldn't give it to Nat all at once, even though that's what she desperately wanted. Natalie yearned to be filled with that massive rod, fucked all the way through with it. But instead, there was a steady rhythm; it felt like Dex was only feeding her the head. She knew there was more. She wanted more. She tried to push back farther but Dex had seized her hips with both hands now and kept her right on that edge.

"Please, please, Dex, please! Please fuck me! Please!" Her cunt, so desperate to be filled; her clit pulsing and ready to explode; everything in her begged for more. "Oh, yeah! Oh, yes. God, yes!" Dex, still moving with the slow grind, drove the cock all the way into her. It felt like a punch deep inside as the battering ram hit her cervix. A firm grip yanked her shoulders back, the force removing her hands from the wall and bringing them down to the floor. Now her ass was the apex of her body and she stretched tautly in three directions at once to keep Dex's cockhead from slipping out.

The next thrust was so deep it made her scream. Or sing. Or cry. Tears poured down her face. Or snot. Or lube. Or come. Wave after wave of sensation buffeted her yet she remained in place, the hinge of her body reaching higher, opening farther. Her cunt convulsed around the huge fucktool that thrust inside her again and again and she began to laugh. She had an epiphany about light turning into matter and she imagined it rolling in her hand like a ball of mercury. She cried out for Dex to please not let her fall, all the while holding her body in this sublime pose that fed her cunt so fully as Dex dove into her from above.

The spasms that wracked her body slowed, then stopped. She was upside down. Dex pulled her upright and wrapped her arms around her body so she couldn't possibly fall. Dex turned her around and they kissed again and it was salty wet. She stroked Dex's hair, her neck, and grasped the strength of her shoulders.

Natalie felt shy to be face-to-face with the echoes of her vora-
ciousness still vibrating in the air. She inhaled to capture the
scent of their skin together.

"I like the way you scream."

Nat didn't remember screaming. She couldn't talk. She
stroked the length of her friend's arm and touched Dex's fingers.
In a rush she remembered the end of yoga, after the straining and
the trembling and the panting and the agony was all done and
Edgar as their beatific conductor had them lie back on their mats
in corpse pose while everything in their bodies and minds was
invited to settle into the ground. She had sprawled her legs open
and exposed her palms to the sky, brushing Dex's hand to her
right. She'd moved a smidge away and had felt warmth spread
across her body when Dex's hand had followed hers, moving
a smidge right back against her hand and she lay motionless,
feeling connected to everything.

"So…" Dex whispered seductively in her ear, "want to go to
yoga with me next week?"

They collapsed into each other's arms, shaking with
laughter.

STUBBORN ACHE

Elena Shearin

I'm watching you while you work, teeth worrying at that lower lip, blue eyes squinted in concentration. Your blonde hair is ruffled and standing up in places where you've been running your hands through it, the way you do when you're stressed. You're sitting at the computer and you've leaned back, arms behind your head, to give your eyes a rest. In that moment I want nothing more than to walk over to you and slip into your lap, straddling those muscular thighs. So I do. Facing you, I rock slowly against you, coming close for tiny closed-mouthed kisses and leaning back slightly to let you see my breasts, nipples perked in anticipation. Your hands are hot on my back, not a sign of arousal so much as your normal body temperature. My body holds no mystery for you; you always know exactly where to stroke or bite or suck to make me push up against you, to make the moisture spread between my legs.

This time I've decided I'm not playing it easy; I'm not going to let you put the puzzle pieces of my orgasm together so quickly, so arrogantly. This time you're going to have to work for it. So I pull back, teasing, shifting as you reach for the waist of my jeans. I can tell that I surprise you when I don't arch eagerly into your hands. I turn to give you a nice view of my rear, firm and round, as I walk away from you. Your surprise prevents you from immediately reaching for me and I make it almost to the bedroom before you move. At the door, I realize you've recovered when I feel your grasp at my waist, pulling me to you as you take that last step that brings you up behind me.

"Where are you going?" you murmur into my ear, kissing the nape of my neck.

"Nowhere," I respond, pressing against the front of you and sliding my hands behind my back so that I can stroke the front of your thighs, before taking a step to pull myself away. You're ready for me this time and catch my wrists in your hands to hold them lightly behind my back. I tug against them and feel you tighten your hold. You press your right thigh between my legs and maneuver me through the door, shutting it behind you and pressing me to the wall beside it. I have my head turned, one ear against wood, the other open, catching every sound of your breath, your voice.

"I said, where are you going?" you whisper again into my ear. A delicious tremor works its way down my spine at the feel of your warm mouth so close to my skin...but I'm not giving in. Not yet.

"And I said, nowhere," the smartass in me replies. I hear you chuckle softly, which I assume means that you know what I'm trying to do; you know I'm playing hard to get. It also means that you think I can't do it. My pride stings (I've never been this easy for a lover before); I try to twist my wrists out of your loosely encircled hands while pushing away from the wall. They tighten immediately as you lean your upper body, just *so,* against me.

And, suddenly, I find myself thoroughly trapped. Shifting both of my wrists into your right hand, I feel your left hand slip under my black cotton shirt, running up my side to cup my breast over my bra. Your hand dips inside the right cup, fingers searching for the taut nipple. With your thumb and middle finger you pinch it slightly, just enough to make me gasp as my body betrays me, warmth building at the apex of my thighs. Then your hand is gone, sliding back down my midriff to the waistband of my pants and then inside. You are over my underwear, but I can feel your touch as though it's against my bare skin. Lightly you cup your hand between my legs, right over my sweetest spot and I flush, knowing you feel how I've soaked through the thin lace. You increase the pressure, moving your fingers up so that the tips of them are right over my clit as you stroke in slow soft circles. I stifle an inadvertent moan and feel you smile against my ear, where you've rested your face. You push a little harder and a tiny groan of frustration leaks from my lips but you keep your pace slow and steady. I can feel my climax building, I'm so wet, and yet you still refuse to speed up, to push harder, to touch my skin, so I press myself against your hand only to gasp when I feel it slip away.

"You're going to stay right here, without moving, until I come back." It isn't a question, and I hate the amused tone in your voice. How do you make my self-control so completely dissolve? We both know that I won't move. I will wait until you come back because I need you to finish what I've started. I hear you slide the box of toys from under the bed, plastic scraping against hardwood floor. They shift and thump as you search for something, shoving them around, making purple dildos collide with egg-shaped vibrators. Soon you have what you want, the box is back under the bed and I am aching with anticipation. I haven't cooled off. If anything, I'm hotter. I hear you remove your jeans as I stand against the wall. A minute later, I hear you put something down, then I feel your hands on my wrists again where I've left them resting against my lower back. You lift one, then the other, fastening a purple cuff around each, and I pull them apart hearing the chain that links them rattle. You put your arms around my waist but won't press your body against mine, won't let me feel that delicious weight, while your fingers unbutton and unzip my jeans. Still stubborn, I plant my feet, refusing to step out of the pool of denim. You must have anticipated this small rebellion because one of your hands is suddenly in my short red hair, tugging enough to sting, the way I like it.

"Step out of your jeans, baby," you say to me, your voice warning. I contemplate refusing, but my weak will wants what you're offering so I step out and push them away. With one boot you tap the inside of my foot to make me spread my legs wider for you. I comply, a chill coursing over my skin as I stand there in my underwear and T-shirt.

"Where was I?" you say, as if to yourself, both hands sliding up under my shirt to cup my breasts. Both hands tease until my nipples are tight peaks straining against the fabric of my bra and then you pinch them, rolling them between thumb and forefinger. I feel you come closer, your body molding itself to mine. I notice the hardness between my legs and I know you've put on our strap-on. This catapults my body from slow arousal to desperate need. You see my eyes widen with my reaction before I think to shut them and turn my face away from you, forehead resting against the cool wall. I've amused you again; I feel your soft exhalation as you laugh quietly against the back of my head. Damn you for being so collected, so cool, when all I want to do is strip off the rest of my clothes and let you fuck me. You hold my waist between your hands and move slightly back and forth, and the head of your cock slides against my underwear right where I'm wet for you. I inhale and this time my eyes are closed so that I can feel you better, concentrate on the hard length of you as you move in a way that is driving me crazy with desire. I am leaning forward, letting the weight of my upper body rest against the wall, and I am surprised when you tug at my cuffs, pulling me away from it. You pull me against the front of your body, your breasts pushing against my back, and turn me to face the bed. There is a small bottle of lube on the footboard and you won't let me turn my head to look at you, one hand on my cuffs and the other buried in my hair. Our bed is high, the edge coming up to my waist, and you halt at the side of it, your hands sliding to the band of my underwear to tug it down. I'm too eager to pretend to fight you, and I step quickly out of them.

"So *now* you want to cooperate," you mock me. The irritation flashes again and you must feel my back stiffen because you swiftly put one hand in my hair, the other on my upper back, and push me down toward the bed, giving me no choice but to bend over for you. My face is turned toward the head of the bed, hands up against my back where they remain cuffed. The lower half of my body is naked and I feel exposed as the cool air of the room makes its way between my legs, teasing that spot on me that your hand has so recently warmed. I feel you move and then hear you pick up the lube and pour some into your hand. I hear you slide your hand up and down your cock and it makes me wet knowing that soon you will be pressing it inside me.

"How many times do you think I can make you come?" you ask me. I snort in what I hope is derision, refusing to answer. Any answer I give you will only challenge you to push me past it. You can't let me win even that small battle.

"I think I can make you come so hard, just once, that your legs won't be able to hold you up," you continue as you take the step that places you back directly behind me, your left hand on my rear. I let out a sarcastic laugh; we both know that I'm nearly impossible to wear out.

"Hmm. That sounded like a challenge," you reply and before I can react I feel your lube-soaked hand mixing with the wet warmth between my legs. You slip one, then two fingers inside me and I press myself down onto their thrusts. Certain that I'm ready for you, I feel you remove your fingers and then the tip of your cock is there, your hand wrapped around its head as you guide it up inside me. I try to move myself down onto it, but you are having none of it. You place your left hand on my back, pressing me into the bed as your right hand continues to glide the toy into my body. No sooner do I have it grasped with my inner muscles than you are sliding it back out. I try to follow it but your hand is still on my back and I grit my teeth. I need you. Now. But you won't be hurried and you settle into a steady rhythm, sliding into me and out again before I can clench myself tightly around you. I'm panting, biting my tongue to keep silent, a childish attempt to keep you from hearing the moans you know are trying to pour from me with every stroke. You lift your hand and spank the fleshy part of my rear, a small but sharp pain that startles a groan from me. Stubbornly, I sink my teeth into the pink fullness of my lower lip, refusing to make another sound, despite a second and third attempt at spanking it out of me. I can move myself up and down, speeding up the steady pace of your thrusts. I want you so badly my thighs are wet from my desire, and you don't disappoint. You push into me harder, moving deeper and starting a circling motion with your hips that almost makes my knees buckle. I am going to come soon; you know it, and coax me with your words.

"Come for me, baby," you murmur, thrusting faster. I grit my teeth and shake my head against the sheets. I'm not going to make it that easy; I'm going to let it build until I *can't* refuse it.

You sense this and begin pounding into me harder, nearly lifting me from the floor with every inward thrust, panting and gripping my waist for balance.

"Come on, baby. Let me feel you come hard for me. Scream for me, sweetheart." You keep talking to me, knowing how your voice pushes me to that edge. I shake my head again, knowing I won't last much longer. And then you decide to tip the balance. Leaving your left hand on my waist, you slip your right hand underneath me and find my clit. With firm, wet fingertips you press my clit where it is swollen and aching, caressing it in small circles and I know I'm going to come now, there is no fighting it. Spreading my legs a little wider, feeling you pump inside me and your hand stroke faster, I let out a ragged sound that is half moan, half scream and ball my hands into fists as I come so hard even you are shaken by the force of it. My orgasm sets my body trembling, my knees buckling, and I soak your hand and your cock with my pleasure. You continue to pump into me, and I can't keep from screaming as the pleasure ripples through me.

Finally, you slow your thrusts and move your hand away in time to catch me as I sink backward. You keep me on the bed while your hands release the cuffs. You move your hands down my body, from my shoulders to my waist in one broad stroke that makes another ripple shudder through me. Then you put one hand on each side of my body, resting your weight against me, tired in your own right. You kiss up my neck, whisper in my ear, "That's my good girl. I love to watch you come." I'm too exhausted to respond.

You stand back up and slip your cock out of my warmth, stepping away to take it off. At the unexpected removal of your support my legs wobble and collapse, making me slide down the side of the bed to land, hard, on my knees. Then you are there, warm arms lifting me and helping me onto the bed where you climb up beside me, cradling me. I'm drowsy now in the rush of satisfaction. My head is tucked under your chin, my back to your stomach, and as I drift off I hear your voice filter through my sleep-fogged mind, tone cocky as you mutter, "I told you so."

Sometimes it isn't so bad to be wrong.

MAID FOR YOU

Deborah Castellano

After yet another long day at the office, I didn't get home until eight o'clock. I dropped my keys and mail on the table, kicked off my shoes and padded upstairs to get changed for an exciting night of lying on the couch in my Juicy sweats while seeing how much Chubby Hubby I could eat while watching TiVo-ed reality television until I passed out. I was only halfway up the stairs when I heard my doorbell. I wasn't expecting anyone.

"Ding-dong! Avon calling!" I heard my friend Alexa call cheerfully. I went back downstairs and opened the door.

"Alexa, I was just gonna..." I trailed off before I got to describing my exciting evening plans once I saw the woman, eyes downcast, standing behind her. I vaguely recognized her from somewhere, but I couldn't remember exactly where.

"What's all this?"

"Darling, you remember Leah from the Chateau, don't you?"

"Oh. Oh! Yes, she was the one you did an amazing Shibari

suspension... Hold it!" I eyed Alexa suspiciously. "Hey, Leah? Could you, um, give us a minute? Why don't you go to the kitchen and get yourself a glass of wine or water or something?" Nodding silently, the woman moved to the kitchen, quieter than a cat. I waited until I heard the water running. "What is she doing?" I hissed.

"Your dishes, I would imagine," Alexa replied calmly.

"No! Make her stop!"

"You make her stop," she said, with a wide grin.

"Alexa..."

"Julie, you're overworked, your cuticles look like shit and the bags under your eyes are too big for carry-on. All work and no play makes Julie a dull girl. So I brought you a gift."

"A person is not a gift."

She waved her hand. "Whatever. Look, just because you've never done anything super formal doesn't mean you can't." She lowered her voice. "She likes you, Jules, but she's been too shy to say anything. And she loves this kind of stuff. Right now you're her favorite kind of hot mess. You're the kind her little hands itch to help. Let her! Even if she just cleans up your house, she'll be happy as a clam. And you haven't even seen her cute little uniform! Besides, I know she's your type. So just think of this as...a first-date delivery service. It's better for you than pizza." Before I could even open my mouth, Alexa kissed me on the cheek, grabbed her keys and purse and dashed toward the door. "Leah, Julie's super excited and grateful that you came here!" she called to the woman in the kitchen. "Go put on your uniform! *Ciao, bellas!*"

Dumbfounded, I stood in my hall long enough for Leah to put on her uniform and come find me. I opened my mouth to say something, anything. I couldn't find the words because my brain was short-circuited by the sight of her. Her black uniform was modestly cut in the front, showing no cleavage at all. She was demurely covered by the black fabric of her dress, over which she wore a ruffled, crisp white linen apron and a small white bow tie. But what a short dress! My goddess, her black stockings, held up by black garters were visible, showing off her delightfully plump thighs. If she bent over in the slightest for anything...

"I don't know what you like to be called," she said shyly.

I swallowed hard and tried to find my tongue. "You can call me Miss," I said, putting on my professional voice.

"Yes, Miss. Would you like me to draw you a bath?"

"I've never had anyone do that for me; I would like that."

"All right, I'll get it ready for you. Why don't you relax in the living room? I'll pour you a glass of wine and fetch you when it's ready."

Obediently, I sat on my couch and nervously sipped my wine, trying to flip through a magazine. This certainly wasn't the evening I was expecting! But how could I complain, with a dish-free sink and a bath being drawn for me? My heart was racing. Secretly, I'd always wanted to have a service submissive to play with, though I could never find the words to express it. And I had a bit of a crush on Leah as well. Somehow, tricky Alexa knew.

Leah appeared in the doorway, her hands clasped behind her back. "Miss, your bath is ready."

"Thank you, Leah."

"Would you like another glass of wine?"

"Yes, please."

She smiled, not looking up from the floor. "Your voice goes up when you use your Mistress voice. It's really cute."

"I never realized," I said, flustered. Then I laughed, thinking about my handful of experiences. "It's true, I suppose! It does." I headed to my bathroom, Leah trailing a few steps behind. Once there, I tried not to gasp out loud. The room was bathed in light cast by dozens of tiny tea lights and there was the scent of rose in the air, my favorite fragrance. The bath was steaming and covered in a mountain of pillowy bubbles. Next to the bath was a small tray with a few dark chocolates, a tall glass of iced cucumber water along with Clinique eye mask pads. My favorite Victoria's Secret pink silk robe was hanging on the door. Perfect.

"Shall I undress you, Miss?"

"Yes, please, Leah, but I want you to look at me while you do." In the dim light I could see her smile and blush.

Meeting my gaze, she slowly unbuttoned my top and folded it neatly. She then took off my bra, lightly brushing her hands across my back, and slid my skirt and panties off. Her hands skimmed my hips as she got down on her knees, all the while looking up at me.

"Would you like your hair pinned, Miss?"

"Yes, please, Leah. The pins are in the bin over there."

I could hear her take a deep breath as she bent over to look for the pins. It was as I suspected; I could see her deliciously fleshy upper thighs, uncovered by the stockings, and her rhumba-ruffled white tanga panties that left little to the imagination.

"When you find the pins, I want you to put them in your mouth and crawl back over to me, Leah."

"Yes, Miss." She dropped gracefully to her knees and crawled to where I was standing, nude. Gathering my courage, I put my hands in her hair at the nape of her neck and pulled hard, forcing her back up. I gently took the pins out of her mouth and put them on the sink. Pushing her gently but firmly against the bathroom wall, I thoroughly explored her mouth, eliciting luscious little gasps from her as I pulled her tiny skirt up and teased her through her wet panties, circling my fingers around her mound until her knees started to tremble. Abruptly, I stopped my kisses and caresses. Trying not to pant, I turned and stepped into my bath.

"Would you like me to put the eye pads on you, Miss?"

"Yes please, Leah." The eye pads felt cool against my eyelids, a delicious contrast to the heat of the bath.

"Alexa told me that you have been having a long week, Miss. I would like to do everything I can to relax you, with your permission."

I was now certain that she could hear my heart as she knelt next to the tub. Silently, I nodded and waited with my eyes covered. She started by massaging my scalp with a firm pressure and then rinsed my hair in rosewater. The water swished as she used rose-scented oil on a washcloth, running the slightly rough fabric across my shoulders, my back and my arms. The sensation raised gooseflesh all over me, so that when the cloth ran delicately across my breasts, I could feel my nipples tighten in response. She skimmed the washcloth down my stomach, then over my thighs, getting teasingly close to my pussy. The cloth splashed against the water and she wrung it out and put it on the side of the tub.

"Poor Miss," she whispered softly. "To be so tense isn't good for you." Her hands brushed across my wet breasts and she delicately plucked at my nipples, the pressing sensation shooting straight to my pussy. Even in the water, I could feel how wet I was for her. She flicked her tongue against my nipples and I couldn't help but let a moan slip out, breathing hard. She continued caressing and kneading my neck, till I felt limp under her ministrations.

"Let me take care of all that nasty stress for you," she told me. Her hands slid down my tummy, slowly but surely, until I was arching up toward her. My legs parted as her hands found my nub and slid into my pussy, quickly establishing the perfect rhythm that made me pant and moan for her. Her fingers circled my clit, slowly at first and then gaining speed as she thrust her fingers inside me, gaining momentum. The warm bathwater and the cold air on my nipples only increased the sensations building inside me, making my thighs tighten until the waves of my orgasm consumed me. I screamed wordlessly as the world went white and my pleasure overtook me, making me shake and buck against her until my orgasm subsided into small tremors. I took the eye pads off and was still breathing hard as she solicitously handed me a glass of cucumber ice water.

Finally, I could speak again. "Next Friday. I want to take you out to dinner. Are you free?"

She beamed. "Yes, Miss!"

"Awesome," I grinned at her. "Now it's your turn..."

THE LAST TIME

Dani M

We haven't spoken in hours. We're both too afraid to say anything else. Everything that needed to be said was pretty much said. And then some. I'm packing my bags and politely moving out of your way to let you by—watching you to-ing and fro-ing around our bedroom, picking up your belongings as you go.

We are exhausted. Too exhausted to fight anymore. Now come the logistics of leaving the home that we've built together.

We're oddly meek with each other now and both of us are wounded. Your fierce, athletic body moves and shuffles slowly around me...tired and labored. I know you're more than a little bit frightened. I want so much to tell you that I'm sorry. I'm sorry it's all broken down so badly. I'm sorry that it's come to this.

That we're not in love anymore.

What if I wrap you in my arms, where it's safe, and tell you that it's okay? That this can all be sorted out. That we'll be okay.

But I can't. It's not okay. And we won't be okay.

"Do you want this?" I ask, pathetically holding out a DVD I bought for you about six months ago.

"No, you keep it; you always liked that movie more than I did." There's a jibe at my taste in foreign movies. It's a good time to take one, since you probably won't ever have to watch questionable French comedy again.

The subtitles always annoyed you.

Sometimes you laughed, though.

Your comment, piss take or not, is said sweetly, and I see the kindness in your eyes that I recognize so well.

"You liked it, if I remember right? Funny how you told me to leave it on when I offered to put on something else."

Now you really do laugh. Your face momentarily sheds the awful darkness around it and falls into a knackered, but genuine chuckle.

"Yeah, point taken. Well, can I have it then?" You give me your hand.

That little laugh. That breaks me a little bit. I smile at you now, weakly. An overwhelming ache makes itself at home in my chest. My usually powerful frame feels like hollow stone. One more gentle little laugh like that from you, and it may crumble in on itself.

Fighting is the easy part. We've put up a stellar effort, raging and battling into the early hours; watching the bond we created with such love and compassion strain to snapping point.

We don't know where we'll be tomorrow.

"Is she picking you up?" The words rattle out of my jaw, which I find is shaking as I speak, and the air goes against me, catching in my throat.

"No, no of course not. I'm getting the train. Alone." Your eyes roll down and rest on the floor, and I see that they're brimming with tears. Your face is fraught with worry and confusion, and your jaw quivers, uncertain.

Acid rises in my chest. There's a falling feeling that keeps happening. Something's knocking me down and dragging me under. Something's pulling the blanket out from under me. And I keep faltering, every second, in time with my breathing. Drop. Drop. Drop.

I hold myself up. There's a growing panic in my stomach that threatens to pull me into the floor.

You see it and move toward me as if to hush me. And I want you to. I need you to. In your usual, big-eyed and seductive way, you press yourself to me and wrap your muscular arms around my shoulders. You know just how to calm me, and your body is my best medicine right now.

This is my ground. Your high, heavy breasts and soft belly press into me, your face finds its way into my neck and the smell of you calms and soothes me in an instant. The smell of you hits me like some powerful drug, and I start to forget why I hate you.

And then I remember again.

My pride puts up a pointless fight against my body's need for you. I let you come close to me, and you lock yourself to me, breathing me into you. I put my face in your neck, and my mouth finds its way to the beads that you've been wearing since we went surfing last summer. I used to bite on them.

Over my shoulder, hot splashes land on my back, trickling down my tank top. They leave a warm, damp line dribbling down my skin.

How did it get to this?

"Please don't cry, baby." The urge to protect you is a strong one, and it's there now, more than ever.

Your hands run up and down my back, grabbing at my body. You're shaking. I need to calm you now, and get you to relax. *It's gonna be okay.* I put my hands to your face, the way I always used to when you fretted, and you impulsively kiss me. Your wet, tear-soaked mouth presses against mine, and despite myself, my tongue finds its way inside your lips. You moan and lick and lap at me, opening still wider to invite me deeper inside. I just can't stop entering your pretty mouth. It always got me. And it's getting me now. I drink you in and feel the effects of you all over me, and with a measure of desperation that I've never felt before, I taste you like it's the very last time.

It is the last time.

You press and strain against your clothes to feel me, make contact with me. The hardness of your nipples against mine starts to make me feel giddy and sick. It's too much. We have to stop this. It's really not a good idea.

But I couldn't stop now if I tried.

You pull back from me abruptly; your eyes look menacing. They're pleading, and they're violent—and I can't look away.

"Fuck me." Your eyes are black. I've never seen them like this.

I stare at you. Saying nothing. A different feeling is taking hold. And it's between my legs.

Your face grows angrier, and you're scared I'll say no.

"Fuck me...please."

I pull back still farther for a moment and watch you. My hands travel from your neck down the front of your body, moving over your agitated, heaving stomach faster than my mind can process what's happening. Pressing my fingers into your abs, I hesitate for a moment, and then let my hand rest at the button on your jeans. Your breath is hot and damp in my face, and the shaking that you're trying to suppress is taking you over.

"Turn around. And do exactly what I tell you."

The words come out of my mouth before I can think better of them. There's no argument from you, just an escaping moan that signals you're already soaking, and you obediently turn around and bend over the bed.

"Down." I push down hard on your back.

You know what's expected of you, and you don't argue. My big, strong butch needs to be topped one last time. Your back quivers as you become more and more unsure of yourself. Feeling vulnerable goes against your every instinct. I know this. I also know how much you need to. Hesitating for a moment, you try and compose yourself. Then, whimpering softly, you reach down to pull open your own belt.

"Good choice, baby." I notice my own breathing is heavy.

You turn to see over your shoulder and catch my eye with a frantic and longing look. I've seen that before. This time though, it's different. Flashes of anger and rage meet my gaze now. And this time, I'm not going to give you exactly what you want right away.

Freeing your jeans, I pull them down as far as your knees and kick your legs apart. You can't move because of the way I have my legs between yours, so you resign yourself to what's going to happen and press your palms into the mattress.

Sliding my hand into the front of your boxers, I find what I suspected. You're soaking wet. Slowly stroking the hot, sticky juice over your clit, I enjoy the feeling of your desperately hard organ straining against my fingers. I know you could easily come now. But I'm making my rubbing maddeningly light, my languishing strokes toying with your hard-on. I feel the blood rushing to my own clit as I'm pressing and buffing your distressed nub, just enough to really torment you. You buck and grind on my hand, angrily attempting to get yourself off against it. That's not happening this time either.

"You'll come when I'm ready for you to come." I withdraw my slick fingers from your swollen folds.

"Fuck you." You spit at me through clenched teeth.

"Ah, there's my girl. That's not very nice, now is it? You're not fucking me, baby. I'm fucking you."

I smile at you darkly when your eyes meet mine.

"You bitch. Give it to me."

You're not happy. I can't say I'm not. My own clit is throbbing with the need to be inside you, though. I'm holding it together, painfully conscious of the ache that's building up in my belly. You're vulnerable and pissed off, and watching you offer your ass up to me could throw me over the edge and make me come in my jeans.

I bear down on the cramp that's building and feel a throbbing in the deepest part of myself. I have had about as much as I can take of making you wait, and I need to fuck you now.

The room fills with the sound of you gasping as I push three fingers inside your sopping hole. Twisting and grinding them into you, I use the full force of my arm to bury myself in you. Your greedy pussy meets me hungrily, sucking and lapping at my hand. I've always loved how sweet and tight you are. And I love it now, as your small pussy opens over my knuckles, slurping and spilling your juices over me. With my free hand, I push you facedown into the bed, and you obey, taking solace in the softness of the pillow while you thrust back up against my arm.

"More, baby, please."

"Aren't we a greedy girl?"

My girl.

For a second, my thoughts are interrupted by the reality of the situation, and I run my nails angrily down your back. As you cry out in pain, I put my mouth to your skin and lick the sweat from you. I can taste blood. This is my territory.

"Give it to me!" Your arms are erect and pulling at everything in reach. Dragging the sheets beneath you, you press and push yourself out violently to fuck me back. You know I'm gonna make this one hurt.

My jeans are soaked with the wetness escaping from my

boxers. Adding my fourth finger and my thumb, I watch in awe as my fist disappears inside you, and I push down hard on your back, trying to steady myself as the sensation overwhelms my head and my heart. You gasp and suck at the air as my fist rolls and turns beneath your womb. I'm aware of sounds coming from my throat and I'm aware, too, that I'm about to come.

Guttural sounds escape from your chest as you cry out and thrust against my arm. My fist goes deeper into you, pushing you farther open as your tight ridges contract and throb around my hand.

Suddenly, I feel your swollen cunt gushing and spitting into my palm, pushing me over the edge completely. Cum flows over my tightly curled knuckles and down my wrist onto the bed beneath you. My clit finally finds its relief against my jeans as I press against you, and I fall against your back over our bed, for the last time. My fist is still buried in your belly, and you hold my arm to keep me there, rolling back and forth on me softly, lost in your thoughts.

There are tears in your hair.

And on your back.

I don't want to move.

MY FEMME

Evan Mora

I'm standing in our garage, door shut, single bulb burning, which might seem like a strange place to be on a hot summer night in the city. But I heard her, my boi, a couple of blocks away, and I know it's her 'cause the rumble from her engine, the biggest, baddest sound around this organic-Pilates-Prius-loving neighborhood.

"My Femme" is what my boi calls her. The Femme is a 1978 twenty-fifth-anniversary edition, vintage teal-blue Corvette. She's got a 5.7-liter engine and can do 0-60 in 6.6 seconds flat. Not that I care about any of that technical stuff. No. But the Femme sure is pretty. She's got more curves than a *Playboy* Playmate, and she turns heads like nobody's business.

When I'm behind the wheel, T-bar roof open, Farrah-locks flowing, I'm like a straight boy's wet dream come true. Sid calls me a cock-tease, which may or may not be true, but it does make me giggle when boys stop in their tracks and mouth a slack-jawed "Whoa" as I cruise by. A femme in the Femme...

When Sid's behind the wheel, it's an entirely different story. The boys, they give her a thumbs-up and want to know what's under the hood. But the girls—I've seen them, biting their lips and flashing their smiles, wondering who this butch Daddy boifriend is and how they're going to get themselves a ride.

And she's given plenty, I know, in her bad-boy, back-alley, late-night past. But not to me. Never to me. Sid and me, we met in the winter, when the Femme was sleeping peacefully, dreaming dreams of spring. By then, we'd U-hauled it to a tree-lined street in the East End, setting up house like respectable thirtysomethings and sipping chai lattes with the neighbors.

But I'm jealous. It's crazy, I know, but true nonetheless. I'm jealous of all the open-mouthed cries and wide-spread thighs that have graced the inside of that car. I wanna feel the slip-slide of sweat-slicked leather beneath my ass and Sid's fingers pumping into me; I want to fill all the air inside that car with the smell of my sex and the heat of my body and the breathy sounds of my moans.

So here I am, standing in our garage, waiting like a predator to pounce. They're in the back lane, Sid and the Femme, so close I can feel their vibrations. The door begins to rise like a peep show window on my strappy heels, painted toes and thirty-four inches of smooth, tanned legs that disappear under my micro-mini. Sid revs the engine appreciatively, and the sound goes right to my pussy.

The car edges forward with a throaty purr, the tip of her hood coming to rest between my legs. Sid kills the engine and closes the garage door, and for a moment, there's only silence. Then the passenger door opens and I saunter 'round, bending low so I can look inside. Sid has a hard time looking past my bikini top and the ample cleavage on display. I know my boi, and I know what she likes, and I know how to get what I want.

"Get in," she says, voice rough with desire. I lower myself in and close the door.

"Get rid of the bikini top." It lands on the floor, and heat flashes in her amber eyes.

"Show me," she says—*fuck* she makes me wet—and I cup my breasts with my palms.

"Pinch them," she says, and I tug at my nipples until they're pebble hard and I'm squirming in my seat.

"You got anything on under that skirt?" I spread my legs open wide and Sid groans—she's a sucker for a fresh Brazilian.

She leans over me, vintage leather creaking, the subtle musk of her cologne surrounding me a heartbeat before her tongue is in my mouth and her fingers penetrate my cunt.

We kiss, we combust, we go up in flames. I wind my arms around her neck, thread my fingers through her hair, stroke my tongue against hers. All the while she teases me, explores me, testing my wetness with her blunt fingertips, painting them along the length of my pussy.

"Wider," she whispers against my lips, and I inch my ass toward her, one foot on the dashboard, as open as I can be. Three fingers replace two, then four replace three, and Sid fastens her mouth to my breast, licking and sucking the rigid peak until I'm just about ready to explode.

"So fucking wet…" She's pumping me now, the wet sound of my pussy a shameless turn-on.

"I want you to fuck yourself on my fist," Sid says, her tongue lapping up my mewing assent. She holds her hand still, leaving the rise and fall to me, letting me work my cunt down over her knuckles, stretching wide, so wide, until she slides inside. I can feel her hand, and it feels so good, balled into a fist deep inside me. Slowly, she moves, then faster and harder, until her forearm is pistoning into me.

"Now," she says, against my lips, then her tongue fills my mouth once more. I moan, half lost, and slide my fingers to my clit, circling, then stroking in rhythm with her thrusts.

"That's it, baby..." She tastes like salt; her sweat and mine. We're panting instead of breathing, and my frenzied crescendo of "Yes baby, yes baby, oh, fuck, yes baby!" ends with a rush when my hips snap up and my cunt clenches around her fist and I come so hard my back arches off the seat of the 'vette like a bow.

In a minute or five, we untangle ourselves with as much grace as we can, given the confines of the Femme. She reeks like sex, and I know I've got a smug smile on my face, but I don't bother to try and hide it.

"You pleased with yourself?"

"Mm-hmm." I am. 'Cause Sid and the Femme? They're *mine*.

I lead the way out of the garage and back to the house, making sure there's plenty of sway for my boi's hungry eyes to follow. Right about now, she's got a hard-on the size of Texas, but luckily, there are still plenty of hours until dawn.

HOW HE LIKES IT

Xan West

I learned quickly that he likes it when I beg. During our first encounter in that bar bathroom, my leopard-eyed Sir showed me that. He doesn't need me to be on my knees (though he does not object, particularly when I'm focused on taking his cock down my throat). It's not about my shame, or my abject posturing. For him, it is about the frequent acknowledgment of both my desire and his control. He is particularly fond of the word *please,* and truth be told, I love hearing it escape my lips. Just saying it gets me wet. Me begging is not just how he likes it, it's how I need it. I ache to bring my raw dripping need to him, offer it up to him, spill it into his lap.

That's exactly where he wanted me that night: in his lap, aching with need. He wanted to watch me writhe with it, wanted to savor the sight of me begging. He wanted to hold me down and watch me have my desire held against me, until I was burning, sobbing with need. He wanted to grasp his control firmly, and decide whether he would let me get what I begged for. He had described it for me, in detail, watched my eyes widen at the thought of it, my breath quicken with the knowledge that he wanted to offer me to another, while he held me and felt me writhe.

I was his to offer, and glad of it: Glad to be valued so much that I was worth offering to others. Glad to be seen for who I was, my exhibitionistic desires celebrated; to have the opportunity to give myself to him exactly how he likes it.

Sir knew me from the start, knew things about me that I had not even fully seen. He was a mirror to my power and grace, showing me how beautiful I was in his eyes, how gorgeous my pain was, how delicious my tears, how much my desire moved him. That is the best a lover can offer, to really see us, and celebrate what they see. It is a rare and precious thing to be seen and valued for who we are. So often, I had been told I was too much, too loud, too smart for my own good; took up too much space, was too needy, too sexual. Sir had other things to say about my hunger, my desire, my size, my power. My reflection in his eyes told me I did not need to hide my need or my self; I could bring it all to him; I could not possibly be too much for him. It scared me every time, felt risky every time, and was exactly what I wanted.

I had not met Dexter before that night. Christian had told me about him, of course. The mentor who had taught my Sir everything he knew about leather; the first transman top he ever met. They had topped together; it was part of learning. But this was different. I was the first girl that my Sir was going to offer to Dexter after seven years of estrangement.

Dexter was on the staff of the kink conference in DC. We came out a day early because of this. We had a room in the conference hotel, and as I unpacked for us, Sir made final arrangements. I ate before he came, ordered the room service, set up the cigars on the balcony, and dressed to Sir's specifications, my hands fumbling and nervous as I attached my garters, my eyes wide as I saw my reflection. I looked like an offering, my hair curling around my shoulders, my small tits raised and bursting out of the tiny shirt, boots drawing attention to the fishnet stockings, skirt short enough to just reveal the tops of the garters. I had been preparing for this all afternoon, luxuriating in a bath, rubbing lotion on my skin, trimming and primping and readying myself, down to the small plug I slid into my ass. By the time he arrived, I felt grounded in myself and who I was, and my body was preparing his welcome in anticipation.

He stalked in with quiet power, greeting Sir with warmth, taking his time to look me up and down. His eyes were feline too, and I could feel my back arch a bit under his gaze. I was ready for him that minute, ached to drop to my knees before him, could not take my eyes off of him. But first there was dinner, and my job to serve it, to allow these men to touch me as I served.

After dinner, there were cigars on the balcony, and me holding the ashtray on my now bare chest, my back to the world, their voices winding with the smoke around me, wrapping round my bare skin, sliding between my thighs. I could tell that Sir was pleased with me by the way he absently rested his boot on my thigh, knew that he was happy to sit here with Dexter, catching up, and showing me off. Every time Dexter chuckled, my clit would pulse, my ass would clench around the plug and my lips would part with a sigh.

I was aching already and they had barely acknowledged me. How would I survive the full attention of both of them?

Sir turned to Dexter with a sly smile, and said, "Shall I prepare her for you?"

Dexter nodded, and took the ashtray from my chest.

My heart started racing. Sir walked ahead of me, giving the hand signal to crawl, and so I did, Dexter's eyes on my ass as I left the balcony.

I approached Sir slowly, with that catlike crawl he loves so much. He was on the bed, and as my eyes met his, a shock jumped between us. He reached down, pulling me by my hair and bending me over his lap. It felt so good to be there, his hands all over my skin, my head hanging over the side of the bed.

Then I felt it. That squirmy twisting as he pulled the plug out. I am never prepared for it, but when it comes as a surprise it grabs onto the center of my chest and squeezes, bringing a tinge of nausea with it. My hands grabbed for the bed as he slowly slid a new plug into my ass, cold with lube. (I knew it instantly; it was the Tristan anniversary edition plug, the one I drooled over in the store, the one he got me for my birthday.) It is so intense when it first comes in, I literally can't breathe for a moment. My eyes were closed, my head ringing, and then I let my breath out. Sir tapped on it and I shuddered.

It is a shift, to go from the expectation of silence, to the expectation that I will show him my need. I am often tentative at first, finding my voice and movement. He pressed me down onto him, so I could feel his cock against my belly, and my ass clenched in response. It was so full, my hand kept fisting the blanket. Then the baton hit my ass, driving sound from me, garnering me praise.

I held on tight, knowing it would last a long time, each stroke reverberating through the plug, slamming sounds out of me. It felt like a pounding relentless fuck, getting hit with that baton, hard and ramming, and it made me grind my cunt onto him and moan. I forgot everything but that I was on Sir's lap, my ass stuffed full, getting pummeled by his baton. The room disappeared, contracted to my need, which had been building all day. I began to beg, pleading with him to let me come for him, describing how much I needed it.

He told me I had to wait.

I began to whimper, words escaping as I throbbed and thought about his cock swelling under me, picturing my ass with the black-and-blue plug, knowing he wanted my thighs and cheeks to match it, aching for release.

I was lost in my own need, writhing on Sir's lap, when I felt Dexter's hands grip my hair. I spasmed, loud begging noises coming from my throat, until they were silenced by his cock, hard and thick and made of unforgiving silicone. Sir kept slamming the baton into me, and it drove my mouth onto Dexter's cock, his hands holding me there, taking my throat for his own, claiming me.

"I know how much Christian likes the sounds you make. I want to feel you begging around my cock, girl," he said.

I worked to get louder, choking on his cock, my whimpers so loud in my own head, tears flowing. I could feel my need covering my skin, wrapping me up; my cunt grabbing air, aching to be full too; my throat gaspingly crammed. It was so much, too much, building and building inside me with nowhere to go. I began to beg louder, desperate to come, and I could hear Sir chuckle.

"No, girl. You don't get to come until he does. So you better please him."

I began to sob, choking, helpless, my hands reaching for Dexter, grasping for his thighs, holding on, as if I was going to wash away. I looked up at him, eyes begging, throat closing on his cock, needing him to come. I formed the words around him somehow, over and over.

"Please, Sir. Please. Please. Please, Sir."

I didn't know if he could understand, but I said it again and again, taking him into me, aching for him, all my need concentrated on his release. His hands gripped my hair tighter, moving my mouth how he wanted it. *Yes,* I thought. *Yes, use me, take me, claim me. Sir offered me to you, and now I offer me too. Take what you need from me. I want you to have it. Please take me. Please.*

There is no greater high than this, when I give myself over, my need wrapping around another's. I wanted him, wanted to please him, wanted him to use me, wanted to be given and taken, to be worthy for exchange. Sir began to beat my inner thighs, and I wanted to be sore and bruised for him, ached for it, wanted these men to take exactly what they needed from me.

Dexter shuddered in my mouth, growling, his hands holding me still as he thrust, deep in my throat, coming. I closed my eyes and savored it, knowing I had pleased him.

"Come for me," Sir said.

I did, letting it out, moaning around Dexter's cock, writhing on Sir's lap as he continued to slam the baton into my thighs, holding on as hard as I could. It felt so good to come, so right.

I felt limp, as they moved me around, got me situated, ready for the next thing they wanted to do to me. It wasn't until I felt myself being held down and spread wide that I fully opened my eyes. Sir had my head resting on his bare cock, his thighs pressing my arms into the bed. My ass was propped up on a pillow, my skirt pulled up, and Sir's boots were spreading my legs, holding me open. I was cradled between his legs, held open for Dexter, who could see everything. My eyes met Dexter's, captivated, as Sir laid his gloved hand across my throat. *Oh.*

Dexter pulled his belt from his jeans, the sound making my heart race.

"You need to be marked here too," he said, running his hand along the front of my thigh above my stocking.

Yes, I thought. *Mark me.*

"Please," I said, my voice trembling.

Belts reached inside me. The pain invaded, ripped through me, wrapping round my throat and stopping my breath. He did not warm me up, and I wanted it that way. Wanted him brutal, wanted him to claim me without holding back. Wanted to show him how my Sir had taught me to take pain, savor its delights and feed it back to him, tears streaming, moaning for more. I wanted his belt deep inside me, as his cock had been and hopefully would be again.

"Take it for me," he said.

I took him in, tasting like liquid metal in my throat, trembling with the intensity of his belt, and let the pain pour out of my eyes, stream out of my mouth; let my cunt drip with it as my ass clenched around it. I begged him for more even as I screamed, my hands clutching the blanket, safely held down by my Sir, feeling him smile proudly at me.

My thighs were on fire, and the flames took me over, until I could feel my cunt burning with it, my chest hot, and I was begging to come for him; could I please show him how much I appreciated his cruelty, please, Sir.

He laughed, and refused me, continuing to lay pain onto me as I writhed, moaning, sobbing with it, blazing. I begged him not to stop, to please keep hurting me, claiming me with his belt. Saying that I needed it, needed his marks on me. He was ruthless and I shuddered with it, a conflagration of need taking me over. I was in that place where I felt like I could take all the pain in the world, eat it all and spit the flames of it right back, a burning circle between us, for as long as he wanted, perhaps longer.

He stopped. Let me writhe in hunger, aching for him, wanting more, begging him to hurt me. He just smiled his cruel smile and watched me, as Sir covered my mouth and nose with his hand, taking my breath and holding it. He made me come, as he held on to my breath, orgasm exploding in my head, sounds escaping my mouth around his hand. I started to move my head, fighting to breathe. Finally, he let me breathe.

"Thank you, Sir." I said, my eyes locking on Christian's, thanking him for so much more than just the privilege of breathing.

Dexter got on the bed with us, reaching for me, and I could feel Sir relax a little. This was what he wanted. They smiled at each other, and there was such intimacy in it, a thousand scenes, hundreds of nights of shared enjoyment. They had missed each other. It was palpable in the room, this aching hurt in their throats. Together again, after seven years, able to connect again. I was one of the conduits of that connection, I could feel it. I was being offered, and with me came new possibilities.

When Dexter's knees came to rest on my thighs, spreading them even wider, I gasped. Then I felt his mouth on my nipple, subtle, precise, a dozen points of pleasure concentrated together, and I began to writhe. His hand gripped the other nipple, thumbing it gently, and I could not be still. My nipples are very sensitive, gentle touch is intense, and firm touch hurts. He was being gentle, and it made my cunt grab for something, aching to be filled. I was spread wide, writhing and empty, and it was overwhelming, this pleasure so close to my heart. I began to cry.

He moaned around my nipple, and Sir began to stroke my hair, forcing gentleness upon me, making me stay with it. My ass was so full and my cunt so greedy, my mouth formed this O of ache, tears streaming down my cheeks. Sir told me that I could come, as many times as I wanted, as long as Dexter was touching my nipples, and I sobbed, looking up at him, devastated by this. Dexter's hand left my nipple, and instead I felt Sir's gloved hand on my chest, pressing into my breast, just holding it firmly. I came, moaning, begging them to stop; it was too much.

They knew better, and made me take it, as Dexter's tongue wrote pleasure on my skin, and Sir's hand held me. Dexter's hand pressed down onto my cunt, cupping me, the heel of his palm pressing onto me, firmly, and I came again, shuddering, whimpering. He began to suck my nipple, and I begged him to stop making me come, I couldn't take it, it was too much. He didn't stop; I knew he wouldn't, and I couldn't stop sobbing.

Sir began to stroke my throat, Dexter licked a line across my chest to the other nipple, and it undid me. I couldn't do it anymore. Anything but this. Give me pain, force me to take it for your pleasure, fuck me ruthlessly, don't just give and give like this. I began to try to fight my way free, Sir's thigh holding me down, Dexter's weight sinking into me, not letting me free, as he tongued and sucked and tortured my nipple with gentleness, his finger reaching down to stroke along the side of my clit. I held on to the bed as tight as I could, coming, begging them to hurt me, to fuck me, to stop doing this to me, the pain in my thighs from Dexter's knees anchoring me.

"Please, Sir. Please hurt me. Please. I will do anything. Please. Please hurt me. I need it. Please. I can't stand it. Please hurt me."

Finally, he did. His teeth sunk into my nipple, and it was so good. He had me tight between his molars, and ground my nipple between them, and the pain was lightning intense, and exactly what I needed.

"Please don't stop. Please, Sir. Please don't stop."

Sir's hand gripped my other nipple and twisted it between his thumb and finger, and I screamed, so grateful, begging them not to stop.

"Come for me," Sir said.

As I came, I felt the baton sliding between my thighs, entering my cunt. It was hard and cold and slippery and I wanted it deep inside me now. My cunt grabbed on to it, my ass contracted around the plug and my breath caught in my throat as I realized how full I was going to be. I began to beg louder for him to fuck me, now, hard, fill me, thrust it into me. I needed it. He kept it right there at the entrance, teasing me with it, as Sir began to run his nails along my nipples, smiling down at me.

They felt good at first, sharp intense sweetness. But soon they began to just hurt in a tormenting stomach-constricting way. They made my ass grab on to the plug and my skin shiver and I could not stop my toes from clenching over and over, my eyes locked to his, begging him to stop. The baton burrowed into me, and it was so hard. My cunt grabbed for it, spasming around it, and I started to cry. It was too much, too overwhelming, and I begged them to stop. The baton went still inside me, and it was too fucking much to have it there, insistent, the hardest thing imaginable. My ass was full, my cunt stuffed, my legs spread wide, my arms held down, and I could not take it, and yet I had to. They were giving me exactly what I needed, what I had begged for, and I didn't want it anymore, but I still took it. Tears were sliding along my neck, and I couldn't even form words anymore, just whimpers.

Sir smiled down at me, put his hands round my throat, and ordered me to come for him. My body responded before I even thought it, just began to move, wracked with pleasure so intense it hurt, my hands clasping on to the bed as hard as I could. As I came, Dexter held the baton there, not letting my spasms push it out. It was relentlessly wooden and stiff inside me, and I ached to be impaled upon it. He pulled it back just a bit, and pressed up with it, in that perfect spot, twisting it inside me, and I sobbed, begging to come, not sure I could stop it from happening. Sir gave me permission, and I spurted all over that baton, my entire body shaking.

Dexter slid it out of me, smiling into my eyes, and stroked my skin, feeling me tremble. I whimpered for him, eyes begging, lost. Sir fed me water, smiling down at me. Dexter lifted his head to look at Christian, raising his brow and gesturing. Sir nodded, and Dexter gave him a wicked grin.

"That kind of girl, eh?"

"She's very good," Sir said, and the words sunk into my skin, calming me just a bit. "She will do it, for me."

Dexter pulled out his cock and told me he was going to fuck me now, that he hoped it would make me cry, because he loved nothing better than to fuck girls as they were crying. Sir hooked his boots around my thighs, spreading me so wide I could feel the muscles pulled taut. He attached clover clamps to my nipples, and gripped the chain tight, pulling on it so I could feel it tighten the clamps. I stopped breathing, staring at Dexter's cock, not sure I could do it. He scared me, the way he wanted my tears.

Sir told me that I could come as much as I wanted to with Dexter's cock inside me, and that I had to take it for him, for as long as Dexter wanted; that I was his to offer, and I needed to make him proud. He said he would help me, give me pain, hold me down, spread my legs, keep me in his arms. It was my job to take it.

I didn't think I could do it. The slightest touch felt so intense. The steady pull of my thigh muscles, the twisting pain in my nipples after all that, and I could barely breathe. I could feel my eyes go wild, could sense the panic brewing.

He took me. He just rammed his way home, hilt deep, and it felt so right. My cunt needed him. His eyes grabbed mine, his weight pressing me into the bed, my head shifting until I felt Sir's cock curve around my neck.

I was surrounded by them, covered in them; it all blended together, swirling into a maelstrom of sex and need and pain and helplessness and pleasure, as he pounded into me, his eyes holding mine captive. All I could do was let go, give myself over to it. The lightning pain in my nipples, the cock slamming into my cervix, the plug so thick in my ass, the bruises on my thighs and ass aching, Sir's cock sliding along my neck as he began to pant just a bit.

It was a storm of sensation and I finally found my calm in it, letting go of everything, my body limp, feeling myself filled again and again, the center of connection between them; feeling them squeezing into every crevice of me. Sir reached for Dexter, resting his hand in the center of Dexter's back, and the electricity shot through me, slamming me as I screamed.

I writhed between them, caught, trapped, feeling them smash into me, both of them, as Dexter reached for Sir, and they held each other, me between them. It built in my chest and cunt, this intense ache, and Dexter drove it out of me with his cock, Sir yanked it out of me with that chain, and I let it out, pouring from me, sobbing, coming, desperate, losing all sense of ground.

Dexter roared in satisfaction, shoving his cock into me even harder, so fast I could tell he was coming too, pushing another orgasm out of me before I finished that last one, and I was sure I was not going to make it, and started whimpering as I cried and shook my head. He began to growl as he fucked me, ramming into me, telling me I had to take it for him, that he was going to fuck me as much he needed to, and I had to take it. I was sobbing and shaking my head, I couldn't take it, it was too much, too hard, and I couldn't do it. I couldn't let go any more. I had to hold on to something. He was merciless, grinning down at me as I cried, moaning and grinding his cock into my cunt in time with my sobs.

He shuddered inside me, his eyes feral and frightening. I didn't want him in me anymore, he was too scary, too much. I couldn't do it, I didn't know how to please him, wasn't sure he really wanted me to let go. I shook my head harder, crying, and looked up at Sir, desperate.

Sir told me to just let go and take it for him, that he needed me to please Dexter. There was no escape from it. I was trapped between them, helpless. I took a slow breath, and looked up at Dexter, aching for him to tell me what he wanted from me.

"This is how I like it. I like fucking you as you cry. I like knowing that it's my cock that is making you cry. I like claiming your cunt with my cock as the tears slide down your cheeks, knowing you are helpless to stop me. That's my good girl. Cry for me."

I felt the tightness in my chest release. He did want me, he did want me to cry as he fucked me. I could really let go. I wailed, and held his eyes as I did it, feeling his cock ramming into me, letting it all out, showing it to him, feeling how it made him come. It felt so good to let go. He was really going to catch me. I was safe. He leaned over, and slid his finger along my cheek, sliding it into his mouth and grinding his cock into me as he tasted my tears. Then he lifted up, and pulled Sir's mouth down to his.

"Taste her tears on my lips," he said reverently, going still inside me, holding his breath as he waited for Sir to complete the motion and kiss him.

I held my breath too, knowing how much they both needed this, how important it was. I trembled, waiting, trying desperately to be quiet for this moment. Hoping.

When they finally kissed, I was aching to breathe, and couldn't. It was like a prayer at first, and then filled with hunger, and sadness, and so much love it made my heart burst and my cunt explode, and I couldn't be quiet anymore.

They began to writhe with me as they kissed more fiercely,

cocks shuddering as they came, growling into each other's mouths. And after we came, we broke into laughter, falling all over each other, sweaty and joyous, limbs all confused and tangled, eyes smiling.

My Sirs wrapped me up that night between them, holding me as we slept, hands gently stroking me, heads resting against mine, slow steady breath on my skin. They had found each other again, and we all knew that they would not let go this time. It was what we all wanted, needed. They were big enough, powerful enough, and cruel enough, to hold all of my aching desperate need, wring every ounce out of me. And I was glad to be held by them, used by them, claimed by them both.

VACATION

Ali Oh

This is my vacation. It includes waking up at 5:30 or earlier every morning to Jae's screaming nieces, sleeping on a couch because I, in my infinite wisdom, forgot to bring my air mattress, and most of all: stress. The lesser stress of worrying that her family doesn't like me and is judging my every motion, word or thought. (I'm sure they can read minds, right?) And then there's the greater stress of her family having too many people, too little money and certainly not enough time.

Yet Jae and I want to make this our vacation. We've taken time off from work to relax. And we...well...we *can* make some adult fun happen.

It starts in the car on the way back from Orlando, after dropping off her brother's computer for repair. We've been teasing all day—remarks here and there, subtle touches. Jae slapped my thigh while we were waking up. The tension had been building and all I wanted to do was fuck. I said so. I told her we had to make it happen. And she kept saying, "We'll see, we'll see." Which I understand. How, in a house with so many little monkeys, can adults have their own time-out? I've made an executive decision to take it outside the house. Jae is driving and I am so hard that I ache. The blood rushes in and makes me stiff, makes my face flush. I reach my left hand under her seat belt and pull her button loose, slide my hand farther down. There's a sensory aspect, something about just feeling. I feel things I don't usually notice, when I'm not staring at what I'm doing. I run one light finger up and down—she opens out, flower-like and just as soft.

"What're you doing?" Jae always asks this when I'm being especially naughty; especially forward. Harnessing my attraction is not my strong suit, so I hear this phrase often.

"Playing, baby boy." I keep running my finger over her slit. I watch her. We aren't naked, so I can't see her body. I can barely see her eyes for the sunglasses, but I can watch her face. I can feel her tense up every time my finger brushes her clit, like that spot makes electricity just for me. She jolts as I find it again and circle around it with one finger. She grabs the wheel, and I see her knuckles white against the black leather. I slide her between two of my fingers, rubbing on either side. She's wet for me—judging from how much, I think maybe she's been wet for a while. When did it start for her? She moves a hand to her face, puts one delicate finger between her parted lips, a silent sigh held back as my slick finger plays. She's my boy, sure. But there are moments when I see her vulnerability; where I see how much she wants me to top her. This's one of them.

I keep making her gasp. She's supposed to be driving seventy, but she's at sixty-four and falling. Cars are zooming by and I say nothing—I want her to lose her mind. I don't want her to worry about the landscaping truck next to us, the driver attempting to watch. I can't take it anymore—she's so beautiful, and as she gets more slick I can't help myself. I rip my button open, tell her I'm not wearing underwear, start touching myself as I'm watching her at the wheel. I'm louder (I'm usually louder). I start to moan and she inhales sharply. I know exactly what she wants—she need not ask. It's written all over her open mouth, her hands gathered at six o'clock; in the way that she shifts, trying to get my fingers lower, into her opening. She wants me to fuck her on the highway.

"Can you drive?"

"Yes."

I inventory my fingers, numb from the seat belt pinching my wrist. But I don't care—I want to feel her envelop me, come all over me. She feels like silk. I fuck her first with one finger and finally, I hear a noise. A squeak and a whisper. Two. She opens for me and I feel her drip down my fingers. I slip one finger into me. Then two. "Fuck me harder, baby boy." She likes when I play like that. When I tell her how thick she is, how much she fills me up.

I make her come on the hour drive back to her mother's house. She squeezes my fingers and I am so lit on fire, burning so hard, I start to squeeze my own clit. "Baby, I'm gonna come. I'm gonna come all over you."

She never speaks—she never says how she likes it, how she's gonna come, how she's fucking me. She doesn't need to. She's pulling my fingers in now, gasping and checking that she's still driving straight. We come together, all over our seats at sixty-four miles per hour.

"Did you like that, baby boy?"

"Fuck."

We aren't the same for the rest of the day. We need more. We wait until everyone's asleep before I start again. I climb on top of her, wasting no time. But Jae surprises me. Every so often, she wants to own me. And it just so happens that today, I want to be owned. I give in, no fighting. I don't flip her back over after her hand slides under my boxers; I don't make a fuss as she stretches them so she can fuck me hard, three fingers pushing me apart and splitting me open. My baby boy wants to take me, and for once I'm going to let her. I ride her hand, rocking back on her lap, pushing her farther into me. She stops. "I think we need to put you up on the kitchen counter." I'm surprised. She doesn't do this, not in her mom's house. After a whirlwind of movement, I'm perched on the counter tiles, boxers on but stretched to allow her mouth. She wrenches my legs apart and pushes me against the cabinets. Her head is between my legs and I grab a handful of her hair as my blood heats up, and I feel myself get wetter as her tongue circles my clit, as she flicks languidly up and down, over my slit. It's hurried—we need this. We need this so badly that neither one of us is out of her pajamas. This is necessary.

I come in her mouth like a punch and I scream soundlessly into the dark kitchen. I claw at her back, mouth open and wanting to receive her. I'm wishing we had a single toy in our suitcase; wishing she could strap on a cock and I could suck on her until she comes in my mouth, return the favor. I want to unhinge my jaw and swallow her whole—I feel raw, animal. I try, after I stop twitching. I slither off the counter and I want to flip her. To make her mine—own her. But she stops me. "You made a promise." I did. I forgot. I said I wouldn't top her here, not when the screaming could so easily reach prying little monkeys' ears. But she made me no such promise. Without ever discussing it, I turn. I switch my hips out, press into hers. She's facing my back and she breathes into my ear. "Fuck." Her hands are not masculine, but they aren't feminine either. They're strong. Hers. They can cradle me and command me all at once, the latter being a power she usually skims over. Her hand is on my shoulder now, and she shoves; lays me out on the counter as if to say she's not finished yet. I feel I'm dripping down my legs—this is unlike her. But we haven't fucked in a week (and that is a long, long time). I swell again, blood on fire, pounding through every part of me and stopping to make me hard. Is she fisting me? That's not possible. We don't have lube on this vacation. But I feel my hips spread apart, ease open and pull her hand. Three fingers, perhaps. Maybe four. She fills me and I brace myself on the counter, legs trembling. The smooth tiles are teasing my fingers and I wish I could yell, bite something. But I am left to my own devices and I'm holding my scream in my throat once again. I keep pushing back—I feel her directing me, telling me how to move, how to receive. (It is not something I'm used to.) I feel teeth on my ass. I hope it bruises as she bites me—I love being marked. Her tongue slides across, on an adventure to find a spot that makes me squeal, push and beg to be fucked. She finds it as she starts rimming me and I ball my fist, smack the mocking white tiles. I don't know how she touches me, fills me from every direction. But she pours herself into me, somehow. My legs become useless wooden stilts as I come again, arms scrambling to support the weight of two women wrapped in complete rapture and forced silence.

Thank goodness for vacation.

COME TO ME

Ily Goyanes

I wasn't able to masturbate until I turned thirty. Well, I guess you can say I was *able* to masturbate, but not successfully. I couldn't come. The first time I tried I was probably around four-teen years old, extremely horny, slightly slutty and harboring a secret fear that I might be a nymphomaniac. I didn't know much about technique, but I touched my pussy and tried to achieve the mythical orgasm I had read so much about.

My girlfriends would ask me over the years, when they found out about my disability during sex-filled conversations conducted over liquid lunches, how could I *not* masturbate. When I told them that I couldn't bring myself to orgasm, they gasped and laughed, completely incredulous because many of them could only orgasm *when* they were masturbating. I would smile, shrug and repeat my standard line, "I don't know. I just can't come knowing that it's me."

That was the problem, you see. The fact that I was the one touching myself, playing with my clit, fingering my wet cunt, just didn't do it for me. It wasn't a lover overcome with desire for me, it *was* me. And I guess I just didn't desire myself at all.

As I trudged through my early adulthood and countless male lovers (I use the term "lovers" loosely; there was never any actual *love* involved), I gradually abandoned trying to make myself come. I mean, after all, I had only sought masturbatory relief on nights when I couldn't sneak out and get some cock. What I didn't realize until almost seventeen years later is that masturbation is not simply a replacement for sex. It is a form of sex in itself; sex with your *self*. And who should know you better than you? With whom else can you be so uninhibited and so free?

Sometimes I thought the problem was a faulty imagination. I should be able to imagine that someone else was touching me, right? But that wouldn't work either, for the same reasons I could never meditate. I was too grounded, too in touch with my physical world to believe I was somewhere else or with someone else. But that wasn't it either. I just didn't want to have sex with myself.

Occasionally, I put on a good show. As I got older and started having sex with both men and women, I would perform the obligatory masturbation scene for them. Lesbian and bisexual women really love to watch another woman get herself off. Men also enjoy the show, but eventually want to become active participants, before you start to think that you might not need them anymore. It was always just a show, though; a precursor to what I really wanted: to get fucked good and hard and without mercy.

My friends, always a source of inspiration, would offer suggestions. "Have you tried using your showerhead?" Or my personal favorite, "Maybe you should try watching some porn first." What they didn't and couldn't understand was that the problem lay not in the preparation, the utensil or a lack of fantasy—I just didn't want to fuck myself. By my midtwenties, I had tried the folkloric showerhead, numerous dildos, vibrators, porn and all kinds of accessories. I had placed nipple clamps on my tits and fucked myself with an eight-inch vibrating dildo while watching porn, and still...nothing. "It's not you," I whispered to my unhappy cunt, "it's me."

When I turned thirty and had brought my barhopping to a slow crawl, I met Cody. I had never dated anyone like Cody before. Cody was neither male nor female in gender. Cody had a cunt, but that didn't confine her to being a woman. Being "strictly dickly" most of my life, I have to say that my high level of inebriation had a lot to do with our first sexual encounter. And our second. But by then I was hooked. Cody would finger-fuck me in the bathroom of the bar, in the parking lot, and once up against the front door of the bar. She would fuck me hard, the way that I most enjoyed it, and make me come and come and come. She would keep fucking me as I came, telling me how dirty I was, what I slut I was to let her fuck me in public, the humiliating statements making me rupture in orgasm until I saw only white and stars and could hear nothing at all.

I told her I couldn't be her girlfriend, that I wasn't gay. Because really, I'm not. *Fluid* is a better word; *insatiable* an even better one. I just love sex; I can't get enough of it. The fear I had harbored as a horny youth had, in fact, come true. I was a nymphomaniac. But what I was not was a lesbian. We could be fuckbuddies, I said. Nothing more. No matter how good you fuck me. No matter how many times you make me feel like I am weightless and deprived of all senses except for the one emanating from my clit.

We argued. We stopped talking for days at a time, three at the most. But we always returned to our sophisticated arrangement.

The sex was too good not to. I introduced Cody to anal sex, which she had previously labeled as forbidden. I lubed her up and worked my fingers in one at a time, until she was moaning and grinding against my hand, her ass greedy for more. I eventually worked her up to where she could take her own strap-on, all nine glorious inches of it. She would bend over for me like a fag, and I would fuck her like one, pounding my femme cock into her ass until she couldn't stand without support.

We would role-play, another of my favorite pastimes: The cheerleader and the jock. The hooker and her trick. The frat boy and the drunken freshman. Before you label my sex life as trite and cliché, let me continue. We also played circus acrobat and ringmaster. We had beautiful BDSM sessions, taking turns being on top. Leashes, collars, restraints, gags, blindfolds, razor blades, hot wax, cigarettes...anything and everything that we could get our hands on to cause each other pain was game.

One day we were limited to phone sex because I was on a business trip. It was the first time we couldn't get our hands on each other after having daily sex for six months. When something becomes a habit, it is hard to break free. "Are you naked?" Cody asked. I made a joke and tried to change the subject. I didn't feel up to performing and I didn't want to have to act with her when what we had was so real. "What's wrong, baby?" she asked. After revealing myself to her completely, it was hard to keep anything hidden. She picked up on my hesitation. "I just don't do that," I answered.

"What don't you do?" I could hear Cody's tone changing, from sexy to amused and curious. "I don't...do phone sex." I answered, hoping that would suffice. She was too smart for that. "Well, then, just fuck yourself and let me listen." She knew she would get it out of me one way or another. "It's not that," I replied reluctantly. "I don't masturbate."

"Why not?" Cody asked. Finally, a response to that statement without recrimination or ridicule, a response lacking incredulity, seeking only the reason why. "I don't know, baby…I never have. I can't make myself come."

"Hmmm…that has to be remedied. You're really missing out. Even with all the sex we have, I still masturbate a few times a week." I was surprised by this. Why would anyone want to masturbate when she was having life-altering sex on a daily basis? "Really?" I asked, not quite believing her. "Oh, yeah. For sure. You'll see." *I highly doubt it,* I thought, and then begged off the phone because I had an early meeting the next day and the sudden urge for a drink.

When I returned, Cody picked me up at the airport. We didn't stop making out from the baggage claim to the parking garage. Once we got in the car Cody said, "I rented a room close by. I couldn't wait until we got to your house." I silently praised her foresightedness. The first thing I wanted after three days of mind-numbing meetings was to be completely filled by Cody—her hands, her cock, her mouth. I wanted to be completely consumed by her desire for me. If I thought it would have resulted in anything worthwhile, I would have been flicking my clit the entire flight back under the cheap blanket. "That's great." I said nonchalantly. If there is one thing I had learned from being a heterosexual woman, it's to not show too much enthusiasm.

When we got to the hotel, we took a shower together. We loved taking showers together. It was like pervert playtime. Penetration is so easy when you're soaking wet. And the feel of our warm wet skin sliding up and down each other's body, well….

In the shower, she took me from behind. My hands pressed against the back shower wall, slightly bent over, I relished the feeling of her pumping in and out of my tight ass. I loved getting fucked like this; when my ass got reamed I felt a pleasure almost unequaled by anything else.

After the shower we made our way to the king-size hotel bed. Cody had chosen well. Knowing how tactile I am, she had selected an upscale hotel with delicious sheets. For a few minutes I lay naked, clean and happy, enjoying that "just fucked" feeling. Cody lay next to me and began tracing the ample curves of my body lightly, with just the tips of her fingers. "Mmmm…" I purred. Cody spread my legs open and continued caressing me, trailing her hands across every part of my squeaky-clean exterior.

"Fuck me," I said slowly, still lost in the delectable feeling of the sheets and the ass-fucking I had just received. Cody chuckled and asked me if I felt good. "Mmm-hmm. You know I do."

"Do you know how much you turn me on?" Cody asked. "Of course, I do," I answered slyly. Cody grabbed me by the face and forced me to look at her. "No. Do you really know?" she asked, an intensely serious look in her normally mischievous eyes. I squirmed a little in her grasp. Was this a new game we were playing? Who was who? What was the script?

She kissed me long and hard, rolling on top of me and thrusting her hard, muscular thigh between my legs and against my sex. This was more like it. "Fuck me," I said again, more forcibly.

"No." Cody rolled off me. She put her hand between my legs and started rubbing my clit in that incredible way she does. Almost immediately I was on the verge of coming. I never have problems coming with other people, in fact, I come quite well.

"Touch yourself."

I cringed… No, really? Did I have to? I was so turned on, so ready for one of our usual sex marathons… *Please, please,*

please don't do this to me...

"Do it. It's about time a big girl like you makes herself come." Cody was being mean, and not in a good way. I wanted body worship; I wanted to see that sweet look in her eye when she stopped to watch her cock moving in and out of my cunt. She grabbed a fistful of my hair and turned my face toward her. "Come on. Show me. You are the most attractive and sexy woman I have ever met in my life. If you can't make yourself come, I will lose faith in sex."

Well, this wouldn't do! I reluctantly started rubbing slow circles around my clit and sliding my fingers up and down my slick cunt. I was soaked. "Touch yourself the way I touch you," she ordered me. I began to try and emulate the impassioned way that Cody played with my pussy. She played with my cunt as if it were the last cunt on earth and she would never get to play with it again. The more I thought about it, though, it wasn't so much a feeling of desperation that Cody exhibited when she played with my pussy, but a sense of adoration. And the more I thought about how much she loved my pussy, the more wet I became.

"Yes, baby, that's it. Make love to that sweet pussy," Cody whispered next to me. I had almost, for a second, forgotten she was there. "You have the most precious cunt I have ever known," she continued "and I have tasted, touched and fucked many cunts in my life." I was getting more and more excited, my breathing becoming shallower, and I was actually enjoying my *self*!

"I wouldn't trade your cunt for any other cunt in the universe," Cody breathed directly into my ear. "Your cunt is the essence of magnificence, a work of art, a masterpiece." I inserted two fingers into my pussy and began to fuck myself hard. "Yes, yes..." I didn't know where the words were coming from or what I was saying yes to. At this moment I didn't know anything at all. I was achieving the pinnacle of great sex—an utter and complete lack of thought.

"You know why I came on to you so hard that first night at the bar?" Cody continued her exquisite torture, whispering in my ear. "Because you were the strongest woman in the room. You moved like a lioness prowling the desert. I knew I had to go in for the kill." With these last words of Cody's, I spasmed, my breath caught in my throat, tears came to my eyes and I saw stars.

ON MY HONOR

D. L. King

It was the Girl Scout badge sash that did it, really. I mean, I was a Girl Scout, as a child, and had a badge sash; still do. It's at the bottom of the drawer I keep my jeans in. I ran across it a few weeks ago. It's tiny. I mean really tiny. There's no way I could wear it now. But she was wearing hers. Here she was on uniform night in a Girl Scout badge sash, a pale green short-sleeved cotton shirt and a green pair of boy shorts.

"Are you a good little Girl Scout or a bad one?" I asked her.

She looked at me and smiled before looking down. "I try to be good, Ma'am."

"Based on that smile, I'd say you probably fail a lot. In fact, I'd bet you're a pretty bad little Girl Scout. Where's your hat? You know you're out of uniform without your hat?"

"I lost it. I lost it in the bushes."

"What were you doing in the bushes?" I asked.

"Katie told me she wanted to show me something, but she didn't show me anything, she just put her hand down my shorts.

And then our troop leader called and my hat fell off. In the bushes." She smiled and ground her toe into the floor, looking up to see if she was having the proper effect on me.

"Just as I thought, you are a bad little Girl Scout. Where did you get the badge sash?"

"It's mine, Ma'am. I mean, it really is mine. I was a Girl Scout for years when I was a kid."

"Well, girlie, you look just fine."

I wasn't really wearing a uniform. I was wearing my short-sleeved leather shirt, black jodhpurs and black riding boots. I suppose I sort of looked like a state trooper—in some alternate universe. The shirt is something I tend to wear occasionally, when I go out. Really, the whole outfit is a normal night at the bar, with the possible exception of the jodhpurs. *Those* I put on for uniform night. Hey, it worked. All the little girls knew I was one sexy-ass top, and that was all that mattered.

"Let me see that badge sash," I said. "So these are really yours, huh? I had some of these. What's this one?" I asked, pointing to one with a coffee cup on it.

Her attention was drawn to the place where my finger rested against her abdomen. "Oh, that's Hospitality or Hospitality Services, I think. Something like that."

"Yeah, I didn't have that one. Guess I wasn't into service, even then. Why don't you go get me a drink and we can talk," I handed her a twenty. "You can bring it right back here. We'll see if your service skills are still up to par." I saw a little shiver course through her. "Ketel One martini, three olives, up. What's that you're drinking?"

"Tom Collins, Ma'am."

"Tom Collins? God, haven't heard that one in a long time. A retro drink for a retro girl. Well, get yourself another one of those too. Show me what kind of hospitality slut, er, sub you are."

She grinned, licked her lips and headed off toward the bar. Actually, she flounced off to the bar, giving her ass a little extra shake, just in case I was looking. And of course I was looking.

The bar was filled with cops, paramedics, doctors and even a few nurses but I was smitten by the little Girl Scout with the curly brown hair, sweet tits and curvy ass.

"Sorry, Ma'am, there was a crowd at the bar. I'll try to do better next time."

The bar looked to be about ten deep in women wanting drinks. "You seem to have deserved that badge in hospitality." I was fascinated by her badge sash. She had a sewing badge and a cup with pens and brushes sticking out of it. I had that one; I seemed to remember it was called Dabbler or something like that. It was an art badge. She had a lifesaving badge and something that looked like helping hands.

"I guess you like to help people, huh? Saved any lives?"

"Nope. I got the badge and then, when I turned sixteen, I passed my Red Cross Junior and Senior Lifesaving tests but I never got a job as a lifeguard. I suppose I do like to help people. I'd like to help you."

I looked at her. "Oh, yeah? What do you think I need help with?"

"Well, anything. I mean, you might need help with cleaning your house or cooking or," she paused. "Or putting your clothes away, you know, like after you take them off. Or maybe I could just help you relax. I'm pretty good at massage—all kinds of massage and I'm pretty good at—providing a canvas for relieving your tensions, ya know?"

I stroked the badges and let my fingers trail down her chest to her hip. She leaned in to me. I could just see the white of her bra peeking out at me. I ran my hand over her throat and slowly moved it down, reaching into the neck of her shirt. My finger traced the top of a cup. "A white bra. How pure and virginal. Just the thing for a naughty little Girl Scout."

We had another round before deciding to go back to the apartment. I'd originally thought a late supper would be good, but when I asked if she'd like to get something to eat, she said, "You mean, like you?"

That did it. I told her she was very bad and would need to be punished and that she'd better come along with me.

"Ooh, you gonna slap the cuffs on me, Officer?"

"I might, with that kind of smart mouth. Hell, I might anyway."

Once back at the apartment, I told her to take the shorts and shirt off, but to put the badge sash back on. It was perfect; she looked like Miss Girl Scout America. The sash separated and framed her tits perfectly. I tweaked her nipples until they stood up and saluted.

"Ooh, Daddy," she squealed.

"I'm not your daddy and I bet he'd be pretty PO'd if he could see you now. I think you'd better stick to Ma'am. Now why don't you get in the kitchen and fix me a nice cup of tea to go with that steaming cup badge you have?" I slapped her ass. I was still fascinated by the way her tits looked separated by the sash.

"On second thought, come with me." In the bedroom I opened my cabinet of goodies. She began to salivate. I took out a pair of clover clamps, joined by a fairly heavy chain, and attached them to her perky little nipples.

"Ooh, Mommy!"

"I told you: Ma'am! You're impossible. Now go in there and make me a cup of tea. I don't think you'll have any trouble finding what you need." I smacked her on the ass again to hurry her along, loving the way the chain bounced with her movements.

While she was busy in the kitchen, I went back into the

bedroom to choose my toys for the evening. I brought an armload of stuff back to the living room, not sure we'd get to all of it, but it's better to be prepared...wait, that's the Boy Scout motto.

By the time my naked little Girl Scout reappeared with a tray containing a steaming mug of tea, sugar and milk, along with a small plate of cookies, I had everything nicely laid out and ready for her. She set the tray down on the coffee table and came over to have a look at everything I'd set out. After fixing my tea, I came back to join her. "What, no tea for yourself?"

"I didn't know I could, Ma'am. You didn't tell me to."

"That's right, I didn't. And that's a very good answer. You won't need to be punished—for that. You do, however, need to be punished for calling me by the wrong name—twice—and for letting Katie put her hands down your pants and losing your hat. A spanking is in order for misbehaving in the bushes. And, just for the record, I'm neither your daddy nor your mommy. We'll have to see what punishment best suits those lapses!" I sat down on the couch and patted my thigh. "All right, get down here now."

Once she was settled across my knees, I fingered the chain attached to her nipple clamps. "Here," I said. "Put this in your mouth, between your teeth, and don't let it fall out." It was a bit of a stretch and she had to tilt her head down a little. I knew she'd be pulling on that chain, tightening those clamps in no time.

As the first smack landed, she jerked her head up and dropped the chain. "What did I tell you?" I picked the chain back up and put it back in her mouth. "And keep it there."

I continued with her spanking. To her credit, she didn't drop the chain again, even though there was a lot of grunting and whining coming from between her clenched teeth. Once her bottom had a good glow going I moved my hand down between her legs. Yes, she was nice and juicy. I briefly let my fingers play in her slick pussy before removing them to her whines of disappointment.

I gathered her wrists together behind her and hauled her off my lap. With both of us standing, I could see that her poor nipples had withstood a lot of pulling and pinching and were red and swollen. I quickly cuffed her wrists and attached the cuffs together behind her back before removing the clover clamps. She squealed and shook her tits when they came off but I ameliorated her pain by bathing each nipple with my tongue and then sucking on it until she moaned. The sheen on her thighs didn't escape my attention.

Pulling her by her bound wrists, I brought her around the couch to the back and bent her over. "Back up. I want those legs spread and that ass in the air. Now, on to the caning."

"Oh, please, Ma'am, not the cane. I'll be good; I promise."

"Oh, I know you'll be good," I said. "You'll be my good little piece of Girl Scout ass when I'm done with you. Maybe you remember what to call me now, but you didn't before. It's the cane for you, my pretty." Just saying that made me feel like Snidely Whiplash and I wished I had a mustache to twirl.

I picked a sturdy cane out of the bunch I'd brought from the bedroom and sliced it through the air so she could hear the whoosh. She shrieked.

"That's right, girlie," I said, and brought the cane down in the middle of her ass. A thin white line appeared and then slowly turned red as she danced on her feet. I gave her two more swipes in quick succession, each just a little lower than the one before, and watched them color up too. A quick peek between her legs told me what I wanted to know. Her trimmed bush had swollen and split open like an overripe tomato. The inside was shiny and wet and the shine was spreading down the crease of her leg onto the inside of her left thigh.

"You really hate the cane, don't you little girl?"

"Mm-hmm," she sniffled.

I pushed three fingers into her cunt and said, "Yes, I can tell how much you hate it."

"Not fair, not fair," she cried.

I pumped her one, two, three times, until I began to feel a slight fluttering in the walls of her cunt. I withdrew my hand.

"Nooo, not fair, not fair, not fair," she cried.

This time, I picked a thinner cane from the bunch and gave her a quick, hard swat right on the spot where her legs met her ass. She raised her hands, as if to reach down and rub the spot, but the leather cuffs prevented her from getting close to the area. Instead, she danced on her toes again.

"Stick that ass out for me. All the way out. And spread those legs; what do you think this is? Rest time?"

"No, Ma'am!" She backed up, arched her back and really pushed her ass out with her legs spread as wide as she could.

I sank to my knees behind her and pushed her cheeks apart with my hands before shoving my face into her wet pussy and licking and sucking out all the juices. I alternated between pushing my tongue inside her and biting her labia before going on to nipping at and bathing her hot, swollen clit—but not enough for her to come. I withdrew my face and grabbed her mound with my hand and squeezed until she danced on her toes again.

"Ooh, thank you, Ma'am," she moaned. "I promise to be good if you'll do that some more." She wagged her butt back and forth.

"Oh, you do, huh? We'll see what gets eaten and by whom," I said. I pulled on her wrists, forcing her to stand up. After I made sure she was steady on her feet, I unfastened one of the cuffs and turned her around to face me before refastening it again, this time in front of her. I bent her over the couch again and kicked her feet apart with my boots. "Push that ass up. How many times do I have to tell you?" I gave it a light smack before pumping some lube into my hand and smoothing it into her ass. I lubed up a large butt plug and slid it inside her. After getting it past the first ring of muscles, her body swallowed it whole, all the way up to the jeweled guard at the end. She flexed internally, pumping it in and out of herself, getting used to the feeling of being filled. "Greedy little Girl Scout," I said.

She whimpered and danced some more.

"Now it's time for you to freshen up my tea. It's gotten cold. Heat it up in the microwave. And I'd better not smell cunt juice on your fingers when you come back."

She pushed herself to a standing position and said, "Yes, Ma'am." She waddled over to the coffee table and retrieved my mug with both hands before waddling toward the kitchen. With each step, her body got more and more used to the plug in her ass. She was walking normally by the time she reached the kitchen. While I waited for her to come back, I stepped into my black leather harness and fastened my double dong onto it.

She came back into the living room, carrying my hot tea, and her eyes grew large. I held out my hand for the cup. "Did you touch yourself?"

She raised her hands, formed the right one into the Girl Scout salute and said, "On my honor, I didn't," then giggled.

"There are condoms on the table. Put one on each of my cocks and then worship them while I drink this tea."

"Oh, Mom—uh, Ma'am!" She raced over to the table to get the condoms. Tearing open one package, she slid the latex down the largest dong and kissed the end. Then she opened a second package and slid the condom over the slightly smaller cock. On her knees, she licked, sucked and kissed the latex-covered double dong while I watched her, slowly drinking my tea. She couldn't get them into her mouth to suck, past the tip of each, so she had to content herself with sucking on the heads and kissing up and down the shafts.

Once I'd had enough tea, I pulled her up by her cuffed wrists and told her to go get both sets of clover clamps. She whimpered but hurriedly rushed to comply. She brought them back to me and I had her bend over the couch one more time, with her legs spread. I attached a set of clamps to her labial lips, letting the chain hang down between her legs, and gave it a little pull to tighten the clamps. While I was there, I twisted the plug in her ass, for good measure. Telling her to stand, I turned her around and applied the other set of clamps to her nipples, putting the chain in her mouth again. "Raise you head, there's a good little girl. Now, trot on over and bring me the weights." When she returned, drool was running down the chain hanging from her mouth and her nipples were pointing up to the ceiling. She handed me the weights.

"Good girl. This time, I want you to put your hands on the back of the couch, bend over, back up and spread your legs. That's right. You know how to do it. Who knows, you may earn a whole new merit badge for this.

Once she was in position, I hung the weights on the chain between her legs, pulling her lips down and tightening the clamps even more. I pushed a finger in her slit to gage her wetness and was rewarded with a veritable flood flowing into my hand. "What a nasty little slut you are," I said, as I twisted the plug in her ass and gently pulled on it. "All this debasement and you're just ready to come, aren't you? Just shake your head, yes or no." She groaned and nodded. "Yes, just as I thought. Lift your head up, there's a good girl." I watched as she pulled her nipples up higher. Then I pulled the plug from her ass and she whimpered.

"Don't worry, girlie, we'll find something to put up there. Just be patient."

She danced from one foot to the other and up on her toes while I retrieved the bottle of lube. I relubed her ass and both dongs. I didn't bother lubing her cunt as it was already wetter than I could have ever hoped to make it. Slowly I lined the dongs up, making contact with her cunt first, as that was the longer and thicker cock. I teased her cunt open and very slowly slipped the tip inside her. As I eased it in, the other tip met her skin. Her anus was still gaping slightly from wearing the plug and it was easy to insert the tip of the second cock into her ass. I pushed forward and up slowly, keeping one hand on her hip and adding more lube to her ass, until the second cock broke through her sphincter and both cocks were fully imbedded in her. She arched her back and pushed against me.

"You filthy, filthy little girl," I chided, as I reached around with a lube-coated finger to stroke the side of her engorged clit.

"Yes, Ma'am. Oh, please, please, Ma'am," she groaned.

"Please what? What is it you want?" I asked as I fingered her distended lips, pinching and separating them before going back to stroke around the sides of her clit again.

"Please..."

"Yes?"

"Please fuck me." She shuddered in my grasp.

"All right. If you think I should. But first, put that chain back in your mouth and lift your head up." She leaned her rib cage into the couch and brought her hands down to the chain hanging in front of her and, once again, placed it between her teeth and raised her head. She lifted one foot and put it down, only to follow suit with the other foot.

I withdrew a little, before sliding back in, then again, and again, withdrawing a little farther each time until I was actively fucking her and had a rhythm going. She pushed back against me and the weighted chain between her legs swung and bounced with each new thrust. She growled when I reminded her to lift her head as I continued to stroke her clit in time to my thrusts.

"You. Dirty. Dirty. Little. Girl. Scout." I said as I pounded into her. "Come for me. Come for me now." I took the clamps off her nipples and, chain still in her mouth, she flung her head back and screamed out her orgasm. I stilled but my cocks remained buried in her while she continued to come. After she'd calmed, I slowly withdrew, leaving us both panting and sweating. I was still in my leathers and I think I was sweating a little harder, not to mention my clit was throbbing in my pants.

I reached down and removed the clamps from her cunt lips and let them fall to the floor. "Damn," I said.

"Oh, yeah," she replied.

"Fuck, honey."

"They should have uniform day every week," she said, and turned around in my arms. "But what about you, Mare?"

"Thanks for reminding me! A little help here would be appreciated. God you're hot, woman!" My adorable Mina kissed me and unbuckled the harness, letting it fall to the floor with a thump before unbuttoning my pants, sliding them down my thighs and pulling my underwear down. She sank to her knees again and buried her face between my legs, licking, kissing and sucking, making all sorts of slurping sounds while I buried my hands in her hair.

She looked up at me. "I love that smell," she said, "the smell of leather and you. Oh god, I think I'm going to come again."

"Yeah? Not until I do, you little slut," I said. It didn't take long. I'd gotten so worked up from the scene I was ready to pop almost from the moment her lips touched mine.

Both sated and curled up together on the couch, I stroked

her hair and said, "You know, there's a company that makes custom badges. I think we should design our own. Like tonight, you earned the Double Penetration badge. It could be a picture of my double dong."

"Yeah, and I earned the Caning badge. It could be a picture of a bottom with a cane striking it."

"Oh, honey, it's going to take a lot more than that little caning to earn a merit badge. But we can work on it. We can work on lots of different ones, like a sewing one, where I sew up your pussy lips, or a butt plug one where you wear a plug all day. You could earn a Medical Arts badge, with a speculum on it and a hot wax badge. Wow, this is going to be fun! And I can earn my own badges too. Like one with crossed canes for a Caning badge and a pair of latex gloves and a white coat for a Medical badge. Oh, my god, the next time we go to uniform night, we'll totally rock the house!"

'50s WAITRESS

Julia Noel Goldman

The television claims it's a hundred degrees out, and it's almost midnight. The air-conditioning didn't work at all during my twelve-hour shift. It was broken on the D train too, and we can't afford AC, so thank god I don't mind the smell of my own sweat. I sit on the couch with the fan pointed at me, in cutoffs and a white tank top, my damp blonde hair in a high ponytail, drinking a dripping Budweiser—it's nice. The simple things are nice. Uncomplicated. I have everything I want. Except what I'm about to get.

More than once today I caught myself smiling at the memory of you on our bed this morning. Just after sunrise, lying on your stomach on the fresh white sheet, your caramel skin flawless, like suede infused by the dawn light. The curve of your ass inspired me all day, reminding me that I am the most fortunate woman on earth, because I get to fuck *you*.

I hear your key in the lock. I listen for the way the Bettie Page figure on your key chain hits the door. I close my eyes as you enter. The sound of your thighs rubbing together through your stockings excites me. Your heels on the wood floor. Your intake of breath when you see me. I feel you standing in front of me and I open my eyes. There you are, directly blocking the television, my '50s waitress, looking as tired as I feel, but smiling. You've got on a gray skirt and a white shirt stained with sweat in the most charming places, and your dark, curly hair is a mess—you look perfect.

"Hey, lady," you say, with the warmest smile.

"Hey. Hell of a day," I reply with my own smile.

"Yeah." Your skirt rides up your thighs as you climb onto the couch and straddle my lap, helping yourself to a swig of my beer.

"Yeah," I say, "but then there's you."

"Yeah. Lucky to feel lucky in a world like this." You finish my beer.

Straddling my lap, you tilt your head down to kiss me and I respond as if I've been waiting all day for this moment. I have. I thought of nothing else. About your breasts and your sexy, cola-colored eyes and about how when I'm with you nothing else matters anymore. Your hair falls into my face as I slip my tongue between your lips, sending little sparks everywhere.

Though I'm sweating, your hot weight feels fantastic in my lap. The delicious scent of you floats up toward me and I stroke your ass under your short skirt—you're not wearing panties, just stockings and a garter belt, and it makes me wet. Yes, life is good. I slide my hands down your damp thighs, back to your butt, over and over as we kiss. Everything is slippery with our perspiration and the touch of your garter belt is such a sexy trip, like you really *are* this bad girl from the past dropped down into my lap for me to fuck. Night after night, year after year, forever.

I don't know why the feeling of you cupping my jaw while

you kiss me makes me so hot, but it does. It could be the kissing scenes in old movies—you *knew* those chicks fucked, but how *could* they, so delicate and proper and well dressed? But you know that behind closed doors they engaged in unabashed, unexpected fucking. At least the lucky ones did.

I squeeze your naked ass hard with both hands and I grind up against you, spreading a trail of little kisses along your neck. My senses are overwhelmed with your reaction to what I've got hidden in my pants, something I put on when I got home, purchased especially for this occasion. You moan and press yourself back and forth against it, leaving a warm sticky trail on my cutoffs. I tell you it feels good. Beads of sweat drip from your hair onto my arms, chest and face, leaving the scent of your coconut hair conditioner everywhere.

My hands snake up to the small of your back and you lean down into my face, kissing me hard as we rock against each other. Our lips wet and slippery, our tongues entwined, you raise yourself up higher on your knees, pulling up my tank top to rub your moist curls against my abdomen. My hands run up the backs of your thighs, pushing your skirt up until it's caught around your waist, cupping your ass, giving it tight rhythmic squeezes. You moan, arch your back, your pussy pressing harder against me, fucking at me. I run my fingers along the tops of your stockings, let them stray into the dark, warm place where your thighs meet, just below your ass. You groan and your legs bend as your thighs part for me, then you whimper as my fingers caress them, grazing your pubic hair from behind, titillating you further. You rest your forehead on my shoulder, panting. So many choices for my next move.

"So, wife, what would you like to do now?" I whisper, still caressing you between the legs, just next to your pussy, the velvet-soft skin of your inner thighs.

"I brought burgers home from work," you whisper as your

fingers open my fly just enough that you can pull my fabulous new hot-pink cock out, bending it in ways I imagine would hurt if it were real. But when you wipe your hand through your come and begin to stroke the length of it, it's more than real enough. I groan as you start slowly jerking me off, pressing the base of it hard against my soaked clit with every stroke.

"Ugh, burgers, yeah, let's just stop now and have burgers," I whisper, stroking your pussy gently, as your come drips down my hand. You gasp. I grab your hips and lower you toward my cock. You ride the tip of it for a moment, your mouth open, your eyes closing with pleasure, rubbing your clit against it. I slip it into you quickly, pulling you down until you are sitting in my lap. You shudder, whisper my name. I keep hold of your hips and begin to move you up and down, thrusting up into you, sure and slow. I stare at your hands as they unbutton your shirt to reveal your fantastic tits in their little black satin bra. I press my face into your cleavage and breathe deeply—like the white stuff in the middle of Oreos, that's what your body lotion smells like. I keep my hands on your ass as I rub my face all over your tits, biting at your nipples through the satin as I fuck you.

"Oh, yeah," I say.

"Oh, yeah? My legs are gonna break off at the thighs if we stay in this position much longer."

I laugh. You wrap your legs around me and I put my hands on your ass, staggering two steps to gently lay you down on the coffee table, and start fucking you again. The pressure of the base of the dildo against my soaked clit is immensely plea-surable, but it's only one of the things that makes me keep fucking you. The main thing is the sounds you make, and after that, how beautiful you look, lying on your back under me, hair spread out around your head, your face flushed with sex. Your eyes are closed and your mouth is open, smiling, making the most erotic little grunts in time with my thrusts.

"Oh, baby, I love you," I whisper into your ear, listening to your breathing, ragged and excited, tiny gasps. I wrap my left arm around your shoulders and rest my head against yours, breathing hard, holding you close, our bodies sliding against each other. My right hand snakes up your side, caressing your skin, moves up onto your breast and stays there, squeezing in time with my thrusts.

"Oh, yeah, baby, just keep fucking me." Your voice is deep and makes me want you more.

I fuck you faster, deeper, dripping with sweat. My cock slides in and out of you, pressing against your clit, against my clit. I bite your shoulder harder than I mean to. I whisper that I'm going to come.

"Yeah...okay," you moan and grab my ass, your feet high in the air behind me, pressing your pussy against me faster and harder, starting to come as I start to come. Your gasps and whimpers send chills through me, my toes feel cold and I come with you, my face pressed against your neck.

Eyes still closed, I kiss you. Your mouth is hot and wet and tastes like sex. "I love you," I whisper.

"Yeah. For seven years now." You laugh. "Happy anniversary."

"Yeah, happy anniversary."

I pull out of you gently and we sit together on the couch, pressed up close, stuck to each other. I reach for the bag of burgers. Life is good.

SKIN DEEP

Anna Watson

Rosa was such a slut that it took her the better part of a year to realize there was a pattern to Terry's disappearing acts: a moon pattern, to be exact. But for a while there, Rosa just wasn't paying attention; so every time Terry pulled one of her no-shows, Rosa would just chalk it up to a bad mood and carry on with her fabulous life. Rosa's postmonogamous, polyamorous motto went something like this: "There are a lot of apples bobbing around in the barrel." She had several players on offer, casual and less so, who were often available when Terry broke a date and who were more than happy to welcome her into their arms (and mouths and cunts). It had taken Rosa no little time to reach this place, physically, spiritually and mentally, and she thoroughly enjoyed being there, often congratulating herself on the sweet fruits of what had been (and continued to be) very hard labor. She had discovered that being a slut, one with manners and morals, was just as difficult as being a model wife.

But once she figured out what was going on with Terry, she felt pretty stupid. Why hadn't she paid more attention? She had felt Terry pushing her away and she had gone off to frolic elsewhere without checking to see what was going on. She had waited for Terry to come to her when maybe it was time for her to go to Terry. Terry, with her suits and her buzz cut, her ripe biceps, her complicated, delicious old-school self. This was not someone Rosa wanted to let drift away, especially since Terry was smart and tender and made Rosa laugh. The two of them had already been through a lot of emotional shit together, pushing each other's buttons, all that. They'd wrestled with monogamy (Terry), emotions out of control (Rosa) and who knows what all, but they'd come out on the other side of it, to a better understanding and a deeper trust. Oh, Rosa liked Terry.

Dialing, Rosa thought, *There are six thousand nerve endings in the clitoris.* This fact always gave her strength. When Terry answered, Rosa said, "Hey, baby," in a way that usually had Terry growling out cocky commands like, "Get your fine ass over here right now, girl, so I can pin you up against the wall and fuck your brains out." Tonight, though, she just sighed and said, "Oh, hi, Rosa." Right on time, by Rosa's count. Damn, she was regular.

"What's wrong, hot stuff?" That got her butch up.

"Nothing! Why? What would be wrong?"

"Oh, I don't know. You just sound a little...achy."

There was a long pause, and then Terry said, through gritted teeth, "So I have a couple cramps, so what?"

Rosa made a low femme croon in the back of her throat, not nervous anymore, going on instinct. Rosa knew, deep in her femme heart, that it wasn't that Terry didn't want to let anyone in, let anyone see her as vulnerable; it was just that she'd been so burned in the past she couldn't admit to herself how good it might feel to let someone in. It hurt too much to believe that someone could minister to her, that she could let go of some of that all-important control.

"You can come over if you want," Terry managed to choke out, then quickly banged down the phone.

"Be right there, baby," murmured Rosa.

When Rosa pushed open the door to Terry's apartment, the butch was sitting on her black leather couch, leaning back, legs apart, watching TV. She was wearing boxers and a tank top and had a studied nonchalance about her: *Who, me, crampy?* To Rosa, she looked like she needed to be curled up in a ball with a blanket over her and Rosa's hands kneading her sore lower back. She didn't suggest it, but she thought at it so hard that Terry shifted uncomfortably and brought her legs together. One knee began to jiggle nervously.

"What?" she barked.

"Nothing." Rosa started to unbutton her blouse, and even in her compromised state, Terry was taking an interest. Underneath, Rosa had on her sexiest bra, her boobies-on-the-half-shell, pink-and-black lace froth bra, Terry's favorite. She was also wearing the miniskirt Terry once confessed had nearly killed her the first time she'd seen Rosa wear it. No panties. Rosa slipped off her blouse and let it drop to the floor.

Terry cleared her throat.

"You look nice."

"Thank you. Gonna invite me over?"

The light in Terry's eyes dimmed and she halfheartedly patted her knees. *Probably feeling too tender for any lap sitting,* thought Rosa. *Poor baby.*

When Rosa was thirteen and had first gotten her period, she'd walked on air for weeks. Her pagan, hippie mom had celebrated with her, making her a moon bracelet with twenty-eight antique red glass beads. They were women together now! Even though figuring out the hardware hadn't been that easy, and even though she sometimes had bad cramps, Rosa loved this longed-for change. Getting her period made her walk differently, her hips moving more, her breasts out and proud, everything about her shouting, "Look out world, there's another woman on board!" But for Terry? It must have been like dying: the death of all her boyish hopes. What did it mean to her now, sitting there, knowing that Rosa-the-femme was profoundly attracted to the masculine in her, and feeling that most womanly of all feelings, the cramping womb, the blood, the monthly disaster? Rosa's whole body softened, and a voice in her head said, *Gentle, gentle,* as she went to Terry and sat on her lap, being careful not to jostle her too much.

Rosa let Terry start. That's how she had to do it, Rosa could tell, if there was any chance of reaching past the hurt. Terry caressed Rosa's breasts, licking and sucking the nipples, lifting each one in turn out of the lacy cups. It felt good, of course. Terry was hands-down the best lover Rosa had ever had, but she could tell the butch's heart wasn't really in it. Slowly, Rosa snaked her arms around Terry's neck and started thumbing those delicate hollows at her hairline. Terry's eyes closed and her hands stilled on Rosa's breasts. Rosa pretended not to notice, keeping her breathing labored and hot, not that she really had to try. Having her hands on Terry, feeling the tremors go through her as she stroked that most responsive and sensitive of all sex organs—her lover's skin—always turned Rosa on.

The TV was annoying with its inane chatter, and Rosa managed to step on the clicker to turn it off without dislodging herself from Terry's lap. Terry dropped her hands to her sides and sank back into the couch. Rosa stroked down her arms, relishing the strong biceps, lingering there until Terry's lips parted, her eyes closed and she drew in her breath quickly, sinking even deeper into the cushions.

"*Mmm*," hummed Rosa. She was wet and juicy and just about now, had Terry been on top of her game, she would have rolled Rosa over and given it to her good, but tonight wasn't that kind of night. Tonight, it was Terry who needed attention, whether or not she would ever admit it. Rosa didn't need her to say anything, at least not in words. Terry's body had been talking to her from the moment she'd walked in. Rosa traced the contours of Terry's left bicep with one nail, gently cupping the right bicep with her other hand. She pressed both muscles with the pads of her fingers, then danced her fingers down the butch's arms, forging a teasing, random trail of sensation across Terry's hands, up her shoulders, around the back of her neck, through her cropped hair. After a bit, Rosa slid to the floor and massaged Terry's calves. Terry shivered and jerked and gasped as Rosa touched her. Her nipples hardened beautifully through the white cotton of her shirt, calling to Rosa, but she kept her distance. Terry opened her eyes once, but Rosa didn't meet her gaze, just let her see the curtain of hair falling over her face as she bent to blow a stream of air over the place on Terry's thigh she had just licked and nibbled. The room grew darker.

After a long, dreamy time, knowing Terry was firmly situated in her manhood now, pulled there in incremental tugs by Rosa's clever fingers, wet tongue and judicious application of pressure, Rosa took her hand.

"Bath time," she said.

Terry's eyes shot open again, and this time Rosa looked. She gazed. She smiled and made another soothing sound, one of those sounds femmes have a whole repertoire of, sounds to soothe the quailing butch. Terry almost smiled back. Then she frowned, looked away and grunted. "But I'm menstruating."

Well, of course she wouldn't "have a period" or be "on the rag" or any other girly euphemism. A little bubble of giggles threatened to burst from Rosa's lips, but she swallowed before it could.

"So?"

"I don't use tampons."

Well, of course not.

"So?"

"The water…"

Rosa didn't say anything else, just placed Terry's hand up under her skirt on her bare asscheek and led her to the bathroom. Terry couldn't help but follow, stumbling a little, loose-limbed and confounded.

"Undress," murmured Rosa as she bent to turn on the water. Terry usually liked Rosa to undress her, but tonight Rosa thought she wouldn't want that particular intimacy. Kneeling, Rosa ran the bath, poured in bubble bath, laid out the ball made of netting her niece called a "ballerina," the liquid soap, the sugar scrub. Then she reached behind her without turning and Terry took her hand and quickly stepped in. Bubbles covered her lower half as Rosa gently pushed her head forward and began kissing the back of her neck until she relaxed slightly. Rosa kissed some more until Terry was holding the sides of the bath as if she was afraid she would slide completely under. Rosa soaped up the ballerina and lathered Terry's back, up and down, side to side. Terry's leg jerked as Rosa hit a particularly sensitive spot, and water splashed in Rosa's face. Terry opened her eyes and grinned.

"You have a mustache!" She gently wiped suds from Rosa's upper lip, and Rosa could feel a shift: Terry was starting to want to take the wheel. Rosa leaned in and let Terry kiss her, and their tongues danced and wrestled until the pressure of Rosa's hands on Terry's shoulders made her gasp, draw back, surrender to the massage. Rosa opened the sugar scrub, loving the nasty texture as she stuck her finger in: it was oily and gritty and smelled of sandalwood and roses. She slathered some on Terry's arms and circled first one and then the other with both hands, slowly down, slowly up, turning and twisting along the way, stopping to draw her nails through the sludge. Both of them were panting. Rosa slopped more scrub on Terry's back and got into the bath, not bothering to undress. Her skirt floated up as she slotted her body to Terry's, the feel of Terry's strong back against her sensitized nipples exquisite. She rubbed her tits through the sugar scrub, her hands around Terry's waist for purchase. From there, she moved her hands around, finally finding Terry's lower back with her knuckles and palms.

The ballerina floated by and Rosa loaded it with liquid soap, reaching around and massaging the front of Terry's shoulders, her pecs, her small breasts with those long nipples she loved to suck; down her belly, her hips, back around to the top of her ass. More soap, and then Rosa dipped; she took the plunge, down the crack of Terry's ass, holding her firmly, her face pressed against her shoulder, cemented to her with glop. And then, after a long, lingering hug, Rosa detached and swished and splashed her way around front so they were facing each other. She washed Terry's feet and toes, ankles and calves, her strong thighs, and then, for the first time ever, she touched her butch. There. Terry went very still, then pushed up against Rosa, all at once, so hard that they both almost went under. Now Terry was stretched out the length of the tub, her head resting on the back slope, propped up by the smooth porcelain, eyes closed. Rosa just kept up her gentle washing. *Just washing,* she thought, and then she said it out loud, softly, into Terry's shoulder. Terry gave the smallest of nods and her body tensed as the ballerina moved. Rosa felt the coiled energy, the start of something. How many times had Rosa been here, between a lover's legs, jonesing for their pleasure, their cum, but now, right now, both Rosa and Terry hesitated at the same moment, and in that moment, Rosa could feel Terry withdraw. Terry closed her legs, pulling Rosa close, and they stayed holding each other until the water was cold. Maybe they were both crying. Maybe only one of them was.

After a long time, they showered together, then Rosa left to slip into bed. She could hear Terry getting a pad, getting set up. When the butch joined her in bed, she was wearing boxers but no shirt. An act of trust. Another one.

"Do you want me to fuck you?" Terry asked, always the gentleman, although Rosa could hear the fatigue in her voice, feel how her body longed for rest.

"Yes," said Rosa, and Terry began to reach under the bed for her dick. "Tomorrow." And as Rosa's fingers again reached to soothe Terry's lower back, the butch sighed, and allowed herself to relax into sleep.

ENVY

Lulu LaFramboise

Your car is like your cock, you've always said. You do the driving, precise and fast, and I never touch a thing. Except I also climb inside the machine of us, and sometimes I give directions.

I knew when I first saw your hands how many girls you'd fucked, and also that I would be your last. You held my gaze for that extra moment, but I held yours for longer. I had you.

What I mean: I follow your commands in bed, but you know what I want, and I know how to soothe you. An example: the time you had me place an ad online. I would be a good girl; Daddy spank me; only phone sex please. It was the men who responded, the dirty grunting fools, and they called me names while I slowly spread my legs wide upon our bed. The best one didn't know he was on speakerphone as he ordered me to worship him, to wait to touch myself until he said the word. I didn't have to wait: you were already slapping my inner thighs with the palm of your hand, letting your fingers graze my clit as you reached back for another smack. Your eyes were blazing as the stranger claimed he wanted me, but it was your dick I wanted inside me, your hands around my throat, punishing me for my indiscretions, this insatiable need for more.

And the caller was getting rougher, calling me "bitch" and "whore," and you mouthed the words, pinning me down. He didn't know your cock was out of your jeans, straining—didn't know you were so stealthy and silent as you bit my chin and pulled my hair. And then you were inside me, the full length of you, fucking me as hard as the stranger claimed to be. We could hear him jacking off, and you matched your thrusts to his, your hip bones slamming my ass, your eyes wild and mean for all the men, like him, who never saw you at all.

We used him, we did, that man on the phone; we used him up and left him spent and gasping. But your cock never goes soft, and your envy streaks to the horizon. The phone clicked dead and I begged you to stop.

"No," you whispered. "You wanted him."

I promised you then that I didn't, but I'm telling you now that I did. Because there is always a stranger in bed with us, an extra pair of eyes: an ex, a student, a prisoner, a phantom desire that makes us hot. And that night there was the real cock you wanted, filled with the blood and pulse and cum of you—that fierce, unquenchable need. So yes, I wanted him, because you wanted him too.

You flipped me over, bound my hands behind my back with your shirt. I glanced at your chest, shiny now with sweat, your beautiful scars pale crescents below your nipples. I tried to catch your eye, but you were slicing me with your gaze.

"Take me, bitch," you said. "For all the women who wouldn't."

You pulled me roughly to the edge of the bed by my wrists and tipped my ass upward with a slap. I felt the tip of your cock bobbing at my clit as you maneuvered me, pushing my face into the bed, shoving my legs wider and wider apart. I was splayed for you, exposed, my cunt still humming from the sex before. It wasn't enough. You touched me, and I was wet, I knew it, but you accused me of not being ready. You spanked me, hard, on my ass, and then shoved your fingers inside me. I gasped.

"Shut up," you said. "This is nothing."

And then I felt your dick at the rim of my asshole. I bit my lip; did you even have lube? Your fingers—three, maybe four—were working inside me, probing at the ridge where I fall into coming, and I could feel your knuckles at the edge of me, forcing their way inside and your thumb, that sneaky thumb, tucked in close. And then your fist, your whole fist was in me, and I was around you, bucking against you and you were ramming into me, through me, pounding. And then: light. A searing, ripping light, from the base of me, up and through my spine. You had spread my asshole wide with your free hand and forced your cock inside with one hard slam. I screamed, but you jerked back and did it again. Your fist in my cunt pulled me toward you and you fucked my ass with a fury, rearing back and bucking into me, faster and faster.

"Take it, my little fag girl," you yelled, your breath fast, about to come from the friction in the jeans you still had on. "You like it when Daddy fucks you raw. Tell me how you like it."

"I like it, I like it," I whimpered, though I was splintering apart from the pain. "I'm your fag. I'm anything for you."

I could feel your cock and your hand meeting inside me, filling me to bursting, and I needed to come; the endorphins would melt the pain in my ass, would lift me, free me, undo me. I was choking with need. You must have sensed this, because suddenly, you pulled out, and my ass stung with relief. You told me to turn over, and I did, your fist twisting inside me.

"I'll suck you dry," you said, and your mouth was on me like a clamp. Your fist was pounding harder now, doing the work that your cock had performed on my ass. I felt your teeth on my clit, too sharp, and I arched up in alarm, but then you were sucking on me, pulling my clit into you like you owned it, your tongue rough on its tip. I surrendered to your mouth, your fist, the suction that didn't yield until the tears were squirting out of the sides of my eyes, and my heart was stopping with my held breath, and finally, I burst apart and everywhere.

Your car is like your cock, you've always said. But the girl in the passenger seat gets the best ride.

WHEN YOU CALL

Sharon Wachsler

I cry out. She shoves her cock into my mouth. "Give it to me, baby, oh, you need it, you need it." I choke on her soft hardness and suck and open and tears fall down my face for wanting her, for loving her, for giving her this release. Something clatters to the floor as she fucks my face, her hand in my hair, and suddenly she is yanking me off her and reaching between my legs—"So wet, so wet." She slides two fingers in before I can say, "Stop, yes, no, I want more. I was feeding you." Here, like this, my words don't have to make sense.

She wants me and I want to give her all I can. There's so little else I can give. She can take all of me, every hole; she can fill and I'll give. That's why she fucks the water from me, so my cunt is gushing—and yes—"Yes," she reassures, pushing me down, reading my frantic words. "I put the towel down. It's okay. Let go. Give it to me, give it to me." And I fall back and open, and liquid drips from my nipples from her sucking, and my cunt streams onto the folded cloth cradling my ass, and my eyes tear, and my nose runs. I am streaming for her, I am screaming for her.

And then a terrible pause: Whose name did I scream?

And it takes me a real minute—sixty ticks of the second hand—to sift through past lovers, recent conversations, common phrases: Caren, Carla, car, Connie, Con. Con. Yes, she is smiling. She is full of herself and of sating me. I must have said Con or Connie. I slump back onto the pillows. She stretches over me like a bridge and retrieves my glasses from the floor. "Oh," I say, laughing, "so that's where they went. I didn't even notice they were gone. You look so good blurry."

"I can always see you." She taps her temple, then pulls herself away. "I need to take a shower." She is coated with me, everywhere. My hair sticks to my forehead and neck. My ponytail must have come loose. I scrounge for a scrunchie to scoop the loose strands into a knot.

I try to swallow the knot in my throat. I focus on her eyes—handsome, expectant—her glasses too far down her nose. Her lips are moving: "Okay?" She pats my knee. "Do you remember now? In the car I told you I was going out with Caren to that new French film? That I needed some 'me' time? And you said, 'Okay.' You sort of waved it away, like it was no big deal."

"Yeah, vaguely." I said. "Reading all those subtitles would give me a migraine?" It's true. It hadn't seemed important because when she told me, it made perfect sense, then. As long as I know what's going on, I can relax. I trust her. Neither of us trusts me. No, I recite to myself, not me, the disease.

"Yes, I'm sorry." My face burns. *Why do you always have to be right?* I had felt so indignant, enjoying my anger, when I'd accused her: "I understand why you need to go out sometimes without me, but you could at least have told me ahead of time, so it wouldn't feel like you have to sneak around, like I'm some sort of encumbrance—" I'd stopped to swipe the tears and snot off my face. "Like I'm too stupid to understand. I could have made plans, too, you know."

Now she pats my hand. "It's okay, sweetie, it's not your fault." She sighs.

"Don't feel guilty." Just a little. I pull my hand away, pick at my thumbnail. She's patting my hand like a child's. *When this fist is in your cunt, you're giving over to a woman.*

"I don't," she says flatly. "I know I need this. I also need to shower. I smell like work." Con reaches across the couch to hug me, whispering, "I love you," but I pull myself away. *I'm not your charity.*

"Go change," I say. Don't change. She heads to the bathroom and the sag of her spine strikes me: haggard. Where is her swagger? I hear the shower blast, water hitting the tub. "I'll get your coat," I call, my hair pulled back, neat.

I'm sucking her tongue hard in my teeth. "French kiss" wanders into my mind. Why, when, the French are so fastidious and controlled, do they call jamming this organ into someone else's mouth, "French"? My tongue babbles against the roof of her mouth, rolling across her teeth. Enamel on enamel: I love it when we scrape at the rough edges, where pieces of ourselves might break off into each other. I am straddling her, she grunts beneath me and I flatten myself on her, so warm. "Lu—" I start to say, but stop, keep swiveling my hips. "Love," I morph it. "Love, Conileh." I bite her neck. They both loved me to bite their necks. Both fat and butch and computer engineers. Both needed lessons in how to interpret their feelings. I taught Lu to dance with my ass pressed against her groin. That got her onto the floor. Soon Lu wouldn't even leave the floor. Then she left. Connie already knew how to dance. She regrets—regrets for me—that I can't dance anymore. I brought it up once, that I recall. She said, "We dance our own way." But I know she misses moving that way, the right way. I dance on Connie's dick, though. I shimmy all over her. I told Connie to learn to put herself first, to figure out what she's feeling, to fulfill her needs. Now she is, goddammit. Now she's using phrases like "me time."

I flop down to watch TV, loud, even though the noise makes me nauseous. I don't ask when she'll be back. If she'll be back.

Con grabs my hips, pulls me roughly toward her. I feel her dick slithering, bumping inside of me and lean back so it rubs my G-spot. I can't stand how good it feels. I almost fall over. She groans and grunts, pulling me against her, my breasts swaying, hair swinging into my eyes, hips burning from being stretched so far apart (she has no idea how much this hurts, but so much hurts me that I don't tell her; it's too much) my clit banging against the harness ring. God, how I love her.

"*Uhn, uh, uhn,*" she grunts as she drives into me. I open a blurry eye to adore her sweaty face, her intense—almost angry—look of concentration.

She asked me once, "Are you fantasizing about someone else?" Startling. "No. What on earth made you think that?"

"Because you keep your eyes closed." *Do I?* "Oh, I guess I didn't know I did that. You keep yours open?" Before she answers, I know: "Yes, I love to watch you."

"I love to be watched. I love you to watch me," I purr in her ear. She moans. Sometimes I open my eyes to see her watching me. I straddle her lap. Her eyes roll back and I grab her by the nape, pull her in, biting her lower lip. I roll into my mind, my hips rocking against hers. "I guess I just can't concentrate with my eyes open. All the sensation, I want to feel it, with my body."

I know she's there, looking at me. The way into my mind is

with hands and words and sounds, grunts and sighs, and a dick between my thighs and fingers digging into my hips. *Make me yours. Pull me in.* My mind is the safety. The fault lines, too.

"I'm entering this—you—with my eyes wide open," she told me in the beginning. But nobody really knows me until they've entered me, my illness, my life. That, I remember. She tells me we've had several conversations about it—that the illness won't drive her away. Then why don't I remember? Something like that, I'd remember, wouldn't I? She says she wrote it down, but I can't find the scrap.

I'm trapped in the middle of a suspension bridge: I can't believe she'll stay; I can't ask her to keep telling me she will. I don't want her to know that I lose the pieces I write down. She might look at me that way—too much sympathy, like how her friends look at her when they say how good she is, how brave, how strong. They tell me how lucky I am. I know I'm lucky. Why don't they tell Connie how lucky she is? They don't hear her groan or feel me grip her when I come; they don't watch us giggle on the couch or smell my lamb stew simmering on the stove. I know she is lucky, sometimes. Sometimes, I forget.

"Come on me!" she commands. "I want you to come on me." There's no dick this time, the first time; just me and her on the couch, the television on. The film becomes foreign as I climb onto her; she's groaning in time. Just her rough jeans and my yielding leggings, bumping my pussy against her zipper as she grabs me ferociously by the throat, growls into my ear, "Come on me, baby—"

"I don't know if I can—"

She bites off my words. "Come on me, come on me!" She is shaking me, grabbing my ass, hard. "Soak me, I want to feel you soak me," and I scream with surprise as much as pleasure. I'm so turned on by her wanting me that bad that the words alone reach into my cunt, squeeze it free: there are convulsions from my cunt, my stomach, teeth, mind, clench and release, wet heat staining our laps. "Oh, yeah, baby; oh, yeah, oh, yeah," she's saying, pulling me against her, our breasts tumbling together.

It becomes our joke: remote-control orgasm. She tells me to come and I do. Her desire for me is my desire. Is it funny how much power she has over me? For her birthday I gave her a book of erotica. On the flap, I inscribed, *I'll always come when you call.* What if she stops calling? Like Lu, who called me: a burden. No, I correct myself, not me. The illness. Lu stopped calling. "The illness is too much for me."

I don't understand too much. For me, it's always a matter of too little. Too little I can do, too little I can remember. Too little keeping me just crazy enough to handle it. People used to chuck me on the shoulder, "Geez, you're too much!" But that was before. Now it's even more true.

Connie is calling me, my name, and "baby," which I love. That, itself, gets her another shower. I'm sobbing into her shoulder as she rocks my ass in her wide-open hands that can hold so much, pressing me into her lap as I come and rent my throat with her name, wordless. She croons, "Oh, baby, yes, baby, give it to me. Give it all to me." I always do. "I love it when you come on me," Connie whispers. *Then I always will. If you come to me, I will come on you. However you want. How often you want.* Remote control girlfriend. I come fully loaded, no warranty on parts or labor. I am tuned in to her frequency, ready to be activated.

I look at the door. There on the knob is her pebbly wool coat. She forgot it. I totter over, rehang it in the closet. Connie never notices the cold.

* * *

I'm watching "Stars on Ice," remote in hand, when Con enters. Somehow between all the commercial interruptions I've forgiven her for knowing what I've forgotten, because I'm happy to see her. I twist in my seat, "How was the movie?"

"It was okay," she sighs.

"That's a ringing endorsement. I'll make sure to add it to my rental list."

"Caren was getting on my nerves."

"Really? Why?" So there. I put concerned sympathy on my face.

Con flings her shoes toward the boot tray, misses, hits the rocking chair. It sways back and forth, deciding whether to fall. "She talked through half the movie and then she gave away the ending! I wanted to throttle her with her Twizzlers!" I laugh and silence the TV. Con flops next to me.

"You are the perfect movie date, did you know?"

"No, I'm not. I can never keep track of what's going on. Half the time I don't even remember if I've seen it before."

"Exactly. So you never ruin the ending!" She smacks my ass, then grabs a piece of rock candy from the coffee table, knocking the remote onto the floor. The crunch is so loud when she bites in, but Con doesn't like soft candy. With her mouth full of fillings, she tempts fate.

"You're making a mess," I grumble, snuggling up and trying to decide if I've been complimented or insulted. "Well, you wanted to get to know Carla better and now you have." Connie's glasses are at the base of her nose. I push them back up to her eyes.

"It's Caren. Remember, you met her."

I raise an eyebrow.

"At my fortieth birthday party," she sighs.

I wish she'd stop sighing. "Well, there were like a hundred people there—" I point out.

"Thirty-seven."

"Whatever. A lot... Wait! Was she the one who ate all the shrimp?"

"No, that was Sylvia. Caren was the blonde with the long nails."

"You expect me to remember the nail length of forty-seven guests?" I poke Connie in the ribs, tickling her. She's back. Carla was annoying.

"Isn't that the kind of thing femmes are supposed to notice?" she pokes me back, then glances at the TV, eyes widen: ESPN. "What were you watching?"

"Football."

"No, you weren't."

"Yes, it was the Bears against the Blue Jays." I think these are real teams.

"Try again," she smirks.

"Okay, figure skating. Kurt Browning. Yum." I lick my lips. She swats me. "So, what movie did you see that blabby Carla ruined?"

"Caren. *Amelie*. And she didn't ruin it entirely. You should rent it. It's good."

"Oh, bleagh, that's French, right? Subtitles? I'll take a pass."

"Whatever." She shrugs. "I'm tired. Let's go to bed."

"Let's." Plural. I love that. "Okay," I grumble, for show. I stand, then stumble, almost fall. Connie throws out her arm to steady me.

"Do you want me to help you walk to the bathroom?" She looks scared. I hate that.

"I'm fine." I twitch her hand off my shoulder. Why does she

have to make such a big deal of a little stumble? It could happen to anyone. "My legs are just a little stiff from being folded on the couch." I recite my mantra: "I got by before you; I'll get by after you."

"There is no 'after me,'" she retorts.

"Whatever," I shrug, fighting the urge to be mollified. Does she think that if she's not here every second I'll shatter, like an hourglass tumbling off a ledge? "You really oughta get out more. Nobody likes a hovering hutch."

Con scowls at me, opens her mouth to say something, shuts it again. "I'll meet you in the bathroom, then." She turns on her heel.

"It's a date!" I call, over-the-top giddy-girly, but she's already stalked around the corner. I grip the wall for a second, make my way into the hall toward the sound of running water. Water. Shit. Water. "Hon," I call, trying to quell my panic. "Can you check the stove? I think I—"

"I turned it off before I left," she calls back. "I'll buy a new teapot tomorrow."

Damn, damn, damn. The third damn teapot this month. Lu, screaming, waving the burnt-out pot, "Why don't you write things down? Why don't you set the timer? Can't you get organized?" Handing me the receipt—making sure the money for the replacement comes out of my disability check, not her hard-earned one. It didn't do any good to explain, "I did write it down, but I lost the paper. I did set the timer, but I forgot what the 'ding' meant." Rolling her eyes, stomping away. Lovely Lu. Long gone.

Ears burning, my toes touch cool tile. I collapse onto the toilet seat, my hand over my face. "I'm so sorry. I'll pay for it, of course. I'm really, really sorry."

"Whatever. It's only a pot. A fucking ugly one, too." She

snorts, "Ha!" at some hidden joke. "Those big, purple flowers! Oh, god! You put us out of its misery, babe."

"But...but, you picked it out." Startling. I lean sideways to look at her face, slip, right myself.

"Haven't you learned by now that your lover is a genius? It was on sale. Practically free."

"Well, still, I should have paid attention. It's a waste." I'm a waste.

"You should be glad that you didn't get killed in a fire," Con spins, cheeks splotched, eyes bright. "Kettles can be replaced. You, babe, cannot. Get over it." Her voice rough, breaking, Con turns back to the mirror, swipes at her cheek.

Her moods flash past so fast. Where did that come from? "You're upset. Are you mad about the pot?"

"No! Wait—yes. I'm mad that you think I care about a fucking ugly teapot. And I'm scared that I never know if I'm gonna come home to a burned-down house with you dead inside. And you bet I'm mad that you don't see the difference. But mostly I'm mad that I have to keep convincing you how much I love you." Facing me now, tears dropping onto her shirt.

Why does she have to get so melodramatic? "You don't have to worry. Really. I'm fine. I've gotten along this far without burning down the house. I'm not going to die." *You'd get over it.* And the other thing? No. Better not. Yes. "Besides, what do you mean, 'you have to convince me'? I know you love me as much as you can, and if you can't say it—"

"Can't say it? I do say it! Christ!" She pounds the sink with her palm so that bottle of red mouthwash topples toward the drain.

What does she say? I look at the stained sink, the grimy mirror. Maybe I can clean in here, the next good day I have. "You say it?"

"Yes, I do." Her voice softens. "I would think that would be the kind of thing you'd remember." She tucks a strand of my hair behind my ear.

"So would I," I lower my head, sniffling, the strand falling back into my eyes. She tells me how much she loves me. I feel myself turning to vapor, rising like steam above our heads. I wonder how often? I condense suddenly, plummet back down to the toilet seat with a thud. "I know—you're right. I should write these things down. I should get organized."

Connie leans against the sink, her mouth open. "That's... what...I'm...saying?" She draws out each word.

"Well, Lu—"

"Fuck Luanne and the femme she rode in on!" Connie grabs her toothbrush and squeezes the paste so fiercely that it misses her brush and lands in a spiral on the floor. "Which was you, by the way," she adds, applying a fresh squiggle of paste onto her brush with shaking hands and attacking her mouth.

"Easy honey. You'll break a tooth." I try to laugh, but my throat is dry.

"I know you think I'm her, but I'm not." She spits into the sink. "And that's not the illness fucking with your head, babe— it's you."

"It's you, babe! It's you!" Con turns from the mirror where she's buttoning her pressed, white shirt.

Modeling the new red dress I bought for her fortieth birthday party, I execute a careful twirl. The short rayon skirt billows up around my thighs. Con catches me at twirl's end, sliding her hand up to squeeze my ass.

"I guess you like it, then?" I bite her earlobe, tonguing the golf stud. She's got on her dress shirt, black slacks. A silk tie with delicate pink petals lies on the hamper, waiting.

"I'd like this—" she slaps my ass, "in anything—in a garbage bag."

"Well, then, I guess there's no need for finery," I make to slip away, but she pulls me in tight.

"Finery is good, too," she kisses down my neck to the V of the dress, her right hand under the fabric, gliding to my breast.

I gasp, "I need to sit down. I'm going to fall."

Con hoists me off the toilet lid, then pulls me back down onto her lap. "I'm dizzy, hon," I mumble into her shoulder.

"Put your head down."

We roll me over onto my belly, my forehead resting on the cool floor, my thighs across her lap. The nausea and dizziness start to pass as my ass begins to tingle, and a new lightheadedness emerges. Fingers run up and down the backs of my legs, making spirals on each upturned cheek.

"What about the dresses?" I mumble. Not dresses. Guesses. "Guests, I mean"—trying to grab hold of anything: the floor, my thoughts, the cold radiator's foot.

"The guests can wear their own dresses. Christ! I love your ass!" Con's hand smacks my ass; my clit reverberates against her thigh.

Yes, that's true, their own dresses. "There's dip too," I offer. Please, please, hit me again. Her hand whistles down, *thwack, thwack, thwack.* I scream and moan and wriggle. All I see is red, a tent of red around my head. The dress, I realize, she's pulled up my dress. My head is swimming in it. I'm so wet. Too wet. "Your pants," I moan. "They'll stain. What about the guests?"

"Fuck my pants," she grunts. And I do. I hump against her leg; her hands, my ass, all have turned red; I can feel it. I see it in the red around me. Whistling smacks, shrieks piercing air, her hand coming down, coming down, coming down. "I love you," my mind whispers.

"I love you baby, baby, baby, I love you, love you. Uhn!"
It's her—her real voice, sweating out the words, muffled by my
dress. And the high keening, like a siren as she pushes two fingers
in and I writhe and ride, wailing, to the rhythm of her slaps
and thrusts. "Come now!" her voice suddenly rough, pushes me
over. I howl, pulsing against her fingers. I hold her inside me,
letting her feel my power, my inner strength, striated, squeezing.
Finally, opening.

My throat is raw. My cunt is raw. I feel fresh and spent,
together. The tile has warmed beneath my head and hands. I can
still hear the screaming.

"Ups-a-daisy," Connie calls from somewhere above. She's
trying to pull me up to her, but I need to be down, low, on the
ground.

"The floor," I try to unstick my tongue. "The floor is soft."
Soft? No, that's not the word. Smooth? I try to explain, but
Connie understands and is gently lowering me, on my side, to
the bath mat. She places a folded towel under my head and I
curl toward it.

"I need to turn off the kettle before we burn another bottom
out," her voice retreats, the pounding of her feet shaking the
floor. Suddenly the strident call is interrupted with a sharp chirp
that fades into a hiss.

Con's face, puffing, appears above me. "Just in time. That's
why I decided to hurry things along a bit. Sorry about that." She
collapses with her back against the sink cabinet, her legs across
mine.

"Oh, I didn't notice," I murmur, feeling hair in my mouth.
The fancy French twist I'd spent an hour creating earlier has
come undone.

"What didn't you notice? The kettle? Or me hurrying things
along?"

"Either. Neither." I giggle, thick-tongued.

"I'll bet you didn't. Well, we both better find new duds, babe, 'cuz you're wrinkled and I'm stained. Also, I'm wrinkled and you're stained."

"Guess that makes us a good pair." I'm waiting for my head to stop spinning.

"Guess it does," she huffs, hauling me up. "Pair of what is the question."

She guides me to the bedroom where we stare into the closet, trying to figure out how to re-cover ourselves.

"...with me?" Con's brow furrows.

"What? Yes, of course I'm with you." What were you saying though...? "What was that last bit?"

She pretends to bang her head into the mirror above the sink. "There was no 'last bit,'" she grumbles around her toothbrush. "I just suggested that since you're in here you might want to take a shower."

I raise my eyebrows.

My lover waves toward my armpits. "You stink."

I glare.

"Darling?" She bats her eyelashes in a way that looks totally ridiculous and insincere.

"What about you? When was the last time you bathed?"

"Oh, it's been...a while." Her brushing has returned to a steady rhythm. "I'll join you, if you like."

"You just want to get me wet and soapy and have your way with me," I accuse, hopefully.

"Okay," she grins, jiggling the red plastic brush in her mouth. A thin foam of toothpaste dribbles onto her chin and splatters onto the floor. I can see the moisture evaporating as I watch, the foam drying, sticking to the floor, where it will soon resemble a cum stain. Con never mops the floors. They're perpetually gritty. That dried, papery blotch of toothpaste drool will probably stay there forever. I'm fascinated by it. It crinkles around the edges, becomes delicate, like flower petals.

Connie takes off her clothing, steps into the stall, turns on the water. Steam rises. She motions to my shower chair. "Milady, your chariot awaits." I take a moment to adore her body, the layers of soft flesh over hard muscle, her right breast a little fuller, more pendulous than her left. Her eyes. It's me. "Are you coming?" Connie stands naked, streaming, soap in hand, beckoning from the stall. I rise, releasing my hair from its clip. *I always come when you call.*

THE ELEVATOR MAN

Lea DeLaria

I am a hardnosed butch. The kind of butch you don't see much of these days. We have gone out of fashion, like landlines and cassette tapes. Occasionally we pop up when your deck needs building or your Pride Parade marshalling. We have faded into a landscape riddled with assimilation and transitioning, forcing us into hiding or worse, extinction. It is a blessing that my business allows me to dress as I please, in tailored suits and crisp white shirts with French cuffs. I am starched and groomed and mannish. I am the last butch in New York City.

I live in a building not unlike myself. Well kept. Somewhat old-fashioned. You walk past at least four doormen to get to the elevator, where there is a uniformed man waiting to press the button that you are either too bored or too rich to push yourself. I have a lovely view of the park.

I never want for female companionship, nor do I need to be involved. I am a confirmed bachelor. Many a young femme have tried in vain to rearrange the pattern of my life. I will always let them try, because for me the chase is everything. Of course by "chase," I mean *I* chase you. Yes, Virginia, there is a butch top, and I am (s)he.

This femme is a pragmatic girl. The sort of girl who wants what she wants. She will tell you what she wants, no matter what it is, no matter where. I know this because I have been watching her since she moved in. I am Interested. Interested not so much in her, but in who she is beneath that confidence. I can sense a girl who might not be as she appears. I can smell it on her. She is a girl who needs to be taken.

The pragmatic one and I live on the same floor and ride the elevator together sometimes. When we do, I stand behind her so I can take her in. She feels my eyes on her. This makes her nervous.

Today begins like any other day. I wake. I have coffee. I shower and shave. I dress. I leave my apartment. I smile inside when I see her there waiting for the elevator. Again I stand behind her, just that little bit too close. I am conscious of her tension. This jumpiness of hers makes me smirk. It also makes me hard. The elevator comes. We step inside: me to the rear, her in the fore. She takes her place directly in front of me. There is no one else in the car.

"No elevator man," she says. I reply only with my eyes on her. Silence. We are fourteen floors up and the car is moving slowly. I step forward so that I am now fixed behind her, my breath on her neck. Stillness. She reaches out, I don't see where, and suddenly we stop. An alarm goes off. She is frozen. My eyes are on her. We are statues. Motionless. The phone rings. I answer.

"Yes, we're fine," I say. "It just stopped." Pause. "Two." Pause. "Can you do anything about the alarm?" Pause. "Thank you, we're fine." I hang up. All this time she has not moved. She says nothing.

"The system is down," I tell her. The alarm goes quiet. "No

cameras." Long pause. "They have no idea how long it will take to fix." I say this so that she can feel me, behind her, on her neck and as I do, I reach around and start to fondle her breast through her blouse. I hear her sharp intake of air, but nothing voiced. She does not stop me. She does not say, "No." I inch up on her and bring my other hand to her large tit. I can feel the nipples harden as I squeeze them between my finger and thumb. Now she makes a sound, a moan. I know this moan. I have heard it before. She wants more from me. So I pull harder. She backs up against me. I kiss her neck and softly lap her ear with my tongue. She becomes aroused, so I bite her. Again she moans. Again she wants more.

"Fuck me," she demands. I pull her tightly to me. "Patient girls get what they want," I whisper.

I run one hand down her side while pinching her nipple with the other hand. Her breathing becomes static. I reach up her skirt and slide into her panties, forcing her legs apart. She is soaked. "That's what I thought," I muse as I begin to stroke her clit.

"Fuck me," she demands again.

"Maybe later," I tease, then cram my fingers inside her. She whimpers. I pull out as quickly as I enter.

"Fuck!" she sobs from frustration. I continue to caress her pussy.

"Do you want me to fuck you little girl?" I ask, my fingers slipping easily around her clit, then in her cunt and around again.

"Yes." She can barely speak.

"Then say, 'please,' like a good little girl." I smile, knowing this will happen. She is too far gone to turn back now.

"Fuck me. *BOY, please...FUCK ME.*" The "BOY" is all I need to hear. I bend her over, hike up her skirt and jerk down her thong. I enter her like that from behind, thrusting inside her. She pushes back hard on me. I hear her talking: "Fuck me harder, Boy. Get it. Get it. Make me cum." I reach around to finger her clit as I drive deeper and deeper and faster and faster into her. Her cunt tightens around my three fingers then explosively she cums. I continue to fuck her as she keeps on cumming, rolling over orgasm after orgasm. I will not stop. I will not stop, because I want it all. I want all of her cum, all of it. Then, and only when she finally begs me to, I quit. We are again motionless. I hear her pant.

I help her become herself once more. It only takes a moment. Wordlessly she stands, facing me now, the pragmatic girl, the girl who wants what she wants. I pull off her thong and put it in my pocket. You see I want what I want too. I smooth her blouse and adjust her skirt. I kiss her then, for the first time on her mouth. She turns around. I stand behind her a bit too close. The elevator jumps back on.

NECK MAGIC

Nancy Irwin

I have developed a fascination with your neck. I put my hands around it and you immediately drop, like magic, into a submissive space. The look in your eyes says that you've become consciously captive and are waiting for my command. There's something that you want, or is that need?

I used to like to watch you bring yourself down and get ready for play. But most of that time I was busy getting the space set up, organizing bondage equipment, getting lube, gloves, chucks and cum cloths ready. I would catch a glimpse of you in the bathroom, or in the bedroom. I have an image of you, a muscular butch wearing a black long-sleeve dress shirt, open and with the cuffs rolled up—and wearing boots, as I requested. You stood in my bedroom door, looking down the hall toward the dungeon. I spotted you and you looked down. The next time I saw you I had entered the bedroom. You were standing at the foot of the bed with your back exposed and your head down. I meant to enter slowly but I was so turned on by the sight of you that I pounced against your back and wrapped my arms around you. Your submission turns me on.

I like that I don't have to take care of you after. What I mean is that you're a strong person, fully capable of running your own life. You manage construction projects, a complex work schedule, properties with tenants, and maintain a Ford Explorer, a couple of Jeeps and a Harley-Davidson. Oh, and you have a boi devoted to serving you. All that requires skill and dominance. When you choose to submit to me, you do so freely. You give up control for a specific time. I may have the pleasure of sharing some ecstatic moments and the peaceful bliss that comes after. This is a gift you share with me, but it's not mine to keep. You're not mine to keep. All this is ephemeral, like a spring blossom or soap bubble; beautiful, but gone in a blink. What lingers is the possibility of more.

So you like to top, do you? I enjoy the wonderful sensations you give me when you fuck me, gentle, then hard. It's taken me a while to relax into you, to allow you to use your specific bondage on me, be placed in a compromised position and let you fuck me harder than I want, harder than I can handle. I can always say stop. It's taken me a while to trust enough that you can punch me in the way you like, which is a way I like. I just can't always take it. My cunt has to be relaxed. But you're right about something: I don't submit. I enjoy specific pain. I get off on it. I mean, I really get off on it: selective, specific pain. There's more I like that you don't know yet. That's okay. I like what you do know. And we're both fortunate for one thing, which is that there are others who we play with who have different interests and talents to share that give us pleasure.

But back to your neck. I remember running a sharp blade along it, nice and slow. You seemed to stop breathing. When I take my hands and cover your neck you don't resist but stay perfectly still. That time at the play party when I took your tie and used it like a noose against your throat you began to drop, and I saw all sorts of fireworks flash in your eyes, because you weren't at all in a place for submission. But it was happening, uncontrollably—until I released the pressure. Sigh. You asked what I was doing. I said I got distracted for a moment, which was true. I didn't want to take you down, not there. If I'm going to have that pleasure I want all of it, your complete undivided attention. A public play party is not a place you can let your guard down, I've learned. So at a public play party I expect to be the bottom. So long as I can't see a line of people watching, I can float in my own little world, one that I share with you. My guard is already down. And with you to watch over me, I feel safe. Besides, I could pop back to fight in an instant, cause I'm not going that far down in a public space either. Like you said the last day we were in Heaven, we both have to drive. I have to leave a play party walking, possibly riding a motorcycle. I'm not afraid of submitting, because I don't. And I like that you recognize and appreciate that, because it's specific too. If you needed that, we wouldn't have lasted longer than a moth to a flame.

The more you submit, the more I want. I don't want to own you. I want to explore you. How far can I go? What do you really want? Can I go there with you? *Hmm*. I've already learned to be careful. You like intimacy of a sort. But you can shut down without notice or visible cause. I have to be prepared for that and keep myself guarded. Can't fall for you, no. You're not available—after you are. There's a trick. Ha. Caution. I think that's what I should name you. You're intriguing, intelligent, powerful, adventurous. I really like adventure. You're willing to play. But you could shut me out at any time. I must always remember that. Caution.

I'll admit it. I'm intrigued. I put a posture collar on your neck and you changed, instantly. Again, it was magic. While I fussed with rope, finding some thin enough to go through the link at your throat—yes, throat—you seemed defenseless. I ran the rope from your throat, down around your torso and made a double run across your chest, trapping your nipples and then tightening the rope with knots until I had knotted right up to your large, trapped victims, fully secure and exposed. Then I tied your torso to the bondage table in a way that secured your arms against your sides. With that alone, you were captured. In fact, with the collar you were. I cannot imagine you wandering around in public wearing such a thing. You would be way too vulnerable. Either that, or you would be forced to block the magic from your world, which would be oh, so sad. That would be worth crying over. May I suggest you never wear such a thing outside the safety of a secure playspace?

I've an idea I'd like to try, to perfect. I have a design I'd like to work on, that involves multiple pieces of rope laced around your neck, with lengths available to secure your limbs. That was a plan of mine that was never executed, because we found a portable sling to play with, which provided all sorts of bondage points. I was able to rope your neck nicely, using a few pieces: one to tie your right arm, one to tie your left arm, one to tie your torso and one to tie your neck to the sling. Gulp. That was the one that got my clit hard, the one that pulled against your neck.

That was good magic that afternoon. The morning spent cutting lengths of rope from a spool, color-coding them at the ends, was good foreplay. When I tied the rope around your neck you were clearly aroused. I loved listening to your breathing, which was anything but steady. When I tied you into the sling your cunt got huge, like it wanted to jump out of itself. I wish you could see that as I do! I had your boots in the stirrups, with rope around your legs. I had secured your wrists, with some room for movement, against your hips. Nothing got in the way of your cunt—except for my hand, and only when I was good and ready.

You were very ready. Your cunt was dripping. I ran a finger up the length of it and thought you were going to explode. I played with you with the rope. Then I ran my wrist across your cunt. Oh, that was good. More dripping. I thought to be kind but wasn't. I put a glove on and lubed up my finger, then stuck it in your ass. I wondered how you would react. It wasn't what you wanted. I knew that. But it was what I wanted. And that you knew. I fucked your ass gently and you gently squirted. I pulled out of your ass, removed that glove, and then I quickly slid my thumb inside your cunt, then removed it. Nothing but a tease, that was. I watched your cunt throb. I talked with you for a moment. Did you understand anything I said? You nodded your responses. I grabbed the bottle of lube and gave myself a handful. Then I gave you a handful. You were so pent up at that point you had trouble releasing. And then you did. With my fist inside you, you squirted. Then I pulled out and rubbed against the inside of your cunt with my fingers. You gushed and gushed, soaking my boots. I wanted that and told you so. I wanted more. I continued to fuck you and you squirted, even when you thought you had nothing left to give. Your head moved side to side. Your eyes were open but you had a vacant stare. You were flying. It seemed a long time before you reminded me that you had to drive. You were blissed. I was too.

Funny thing that. It's very different fucking you than getting fucked, but somehow, after a really wonderful session like that one, I'm left feeling as high as if I'd been the one in the sling. How can that be? I'm not really sure. Of course you are way higher. It's just that I'm so fucking turned on fucking you, so hard from watching you react to my touch that I end up wetting my pants—when I'm wearing any. What was I wearing that day? There might have been a dress. I know I was wearing boots. That's why it was so much fun to have you squirt all over me. You covered my belly and my legs with your juices, and splashed all over my boots. But my own juices were running down my thighs at the same time.

What are we gonna do next, Max? I know when I expect to see you. Will you let me tie you up again and believe I'm having my way with you, when all the while, I'm doing exactly what you want me to? If it works for me and it works for you, is there any harm in pretending that I'm 100 percent in control and that you've given up completely and entirely for my pleasure? The thing is, the more we do this and the further we explore, the less it seems like it matters. I get to have fun exploring you and you get to enjoy being explored. I rather doubt you will get into trouble. You've got too many people you play with and too many safeguards in place. You do know about those safeguards, don't you?

I know about the not so safe: the rope, the knives, my hands around your neck. More dangerous than that are my words, my commands. Perhaps one day we'll play that way, and there will be no physical restraint. Who would understand that's the most dangerous of all?

NEVER TOO OLD

DeJay

"You did what?"

"I just went online and got the address of Wild Hearts for you. It's on Commercial Street, right across from the Crown and Anchor, so I can wait there and have a drink while you pick up our purchases."

I looked at my wife, my partner of thirty-plus years, and couldn't believe what she had just said. "Why would you do that?"

She smiled at me—the little-girl grin, the one where her eyes twinkle and her dimples pop. "It'll be fun."

"Fun?" I felt like I didn't even know her.

She walked over and wrapped her arms around my neck. "It will be, I promise." With that she kissed me.

"I'm not so sure about this."

"Don't be a baby."

"Why do I have to go? You're the one who wants this stuff."

"Because they have to measure you, silly."

The glint in her eye had me wary. "Measure me?" I thought about that for a moment. "There?"

"No, you idiot, your hips and thighs." After pouring herself a cup of coffee she held the pot out to me. As if everything were perfectly normal, she asked, "Want some more?"

"No. Yes. Fuck." I looked at her closely for some hint, some idea as to what I had been doing wrong. "I thought we were okay in that department?"

She poured the coffee and looked up.

"You know we are."

"I mean, we have sex at least twice a week, sometimes three, right?"

"It's not about that."

"I only fell asleep last week because I was exhausted, I swear."

"Honey, it's not about you falling asleep."

I started to sweat. "I thought, you know, that you enjoyed our sex life." Had she been faking it all this time?

Abby walked closer and cupped my jaw. "Honey, I do. We have a great sex life. This is just a little experiment, something to spice it up, that's all."

"Now? At our age?"

"We're not dead, you know, and I've been thinking about it for a while."

My insides were churning full blast now. "A while?"

"Remember a couple months ago when we had that problem with dryness?"

I thought back, then nodded. "You called the doctor, right?"

"Yes, but I also talked to Mary."

I groaned out loud.

"Stop it. We're all adults, and she and I are the same age, so it was perfectly natural to ask her."

I put my head in my hands. "And?"

"And she had the same problem. Vicky got her some lubricants."

I sat up straighter, immediately feeling better. "We did, too."

"Exactly, but did you know there are many kinds of lubricants? Some even flavored, for…you know. So we discussed that and other stuff."

"Fuck." I looked at her pleadingly.

"Stop it."

"Please tell me you did not discuss our sex life, I'm begging you."

"Grow up."

I put my head in my arms on the ceramic countertop. The day had started so nicely. I woke early, did the treadmill for an hour. I had an idea for a story. I was working at the kitchen counter on my laptop while the coffee perked and the dogs were outside. I even asked Abby to give me quiet time to write, and she had agreed, as usual. Then not ten minutes later she came into the kitchen and made her announcement. I took a deep breath. "And?"

"Well, when Mary and I talked, she told me that she and Vicky, they have one."

"Oh fuck, you did not just tell me that." I rubbed my eyes desperately trying to erase that image of my best friend, with a strap-on, from my brain. "Why do you insist on telling me shit like this, why?"

"What is the big deal? It's perfectly normal."

I took a deep breath and twisted my neck from side to side, still trying to purge the image. "Normal? Absolutely! But, I do not ever want to think of my two best friends like that. Is that okay with you?"

"Why?"

"Because they're my friends, damn it."

"Don't be such a child." She rubbed my hand and grinned. "You can't get the image out of your mind, can you?"

She was right. "No, and I'm blaming you."

She started laughing, then stopped abruptly. "Okay, so it's a little embarrassing, but they're our friends."

"Tell me now, before I ever see Vicky again, did you tell Mary you want to do this?"

"No, of course not."

"You swear?"

"I swear." She crossed her heart. I almost believed her.

"I do not want another incident like when Mary told me about Vic wearing a damn nightgown."

Abby knew I still had trouble looking my best friend in the eye ever since her wife had revealed that little tidbit. Vic, a butch's butch if ever there was one, wore a pink-flowered, flannel nightgown. Fuck, now I was picturing her in the damn nightgown with a friggin' strap-on underneath.

"Don't be silly."

"I'm not."

"So anyway, I've been thinking about it and decided our trip to P-town provides the perfect time for us to get equipped."

"Equipped?"

"Supplies."

I ran my hands through my hair. The world had gone mad, nothing was making any sense. "You're going with me. Why do I have to go in there alone?"

"Remember the Sears incident?"

I cringed. Years ago we had been shopping for Christmas presents. Abby found a robe she thought her mom would like and asked me to try it on to see if the length was okay, since her mom and I had similar builds. There I was, in my jeans, motorcycle boots and a leather jacket. It was a simple, stupid cotton frock with lace around the collar. Once I had it on, Abby started laughing and wouldn't stop. The angrier I got, the more she laughed; the more she laughed, the more she alerted our fellow shoppers, who then started staring and laughing as well. I tore the damn thing off and never helped her again.

"I ordered everything from the catalogue. All you have to do is let them make sure the harness is the right size, and then pay for it and leave. Simple."

Abby stood there angelically smiling. I was sure I was missing something.

"You already ordered what you want, right?"

"Yup."

"All I have to do is check on the size of the harness, right?"

"Absolutely."

"Ten minutes tops?"

"Less."

"What if someone I know is in the store?"

"Say hi."

I shook my head. "You know what I mean. How am I going to explain why I'm there?"

"What do you think they're doing there?"

I covered my ears. "Fuck, I do not want to think about that."

"Stop being ridiculous. I think it's wonderful people our age are willing to experiment."

"Please tell me what's really going on here?"

Abby leaned in close and kissed me. "I don't want you trading me in for three twenties."

Each time she hit another milestone in age, she decided I would trade her in for X number of younger women. At thirty, it was two fifteen-year-olds. I pointed out that would be jailbait.

At forty, it was two twenty-year-olds; I asked what the hell I would do with them. At fifty, she announced two twenty-five year-olds, because I was older and needed to slow down. Now at sixty, this.

"I love you, I can barely keep up with you. Have you talked to a twenty-year-old of late? I don't even understand their language."

"It's not you having a conversation with them I'm worried about."

"Abbs, I've never given you reason to worry, have I?"

She kissed me again. "And I intend to make sure you want to come home to me and only me."

"Now who's being childish?"

"Please, it's important to me."

I sighed, knowing I had lost this battle. "Quick in and out, right?"

"Let's get going, you have a one o'clock appointment with Cheryl."

"Cheryl?" I was towel drying my hair after my shower.

"The store, Wild Hearts."

"I need an appointment to shop?"

"Well, it's their personalized service. I thought you would like that."

"Oh. Okay." I grabbed my T-shirt.

"Make sure you wear boxers today."

"Huh?"

"Just do it."

"Why?"

Abby was applying mascara; she looked in the mirror at me. "So I don't have to worry about you."

I walked toward her, my jeans in one hand, naked from the

waist down. "I thought you liked it when I went commando."

"Not today."

She had been in a funny mood ever since we arrived in P-town. This morning after breakfast, instead of going sightseeing, she had wanted to come back here and make love. I was up for that, but she still seemed edgy.

"Okay. Boxers it is."

Abby grabbed a pair out of the duffle bag and handed them to me.

"You're lucky I packed some," I told her.

"No. You are, or you'd be wearing a pair of my panties."

"Like hell."

She just giggled and returned to putting on her makeup. Once I was dressed, she turned to me. "You look nice."

I was only wearing jeans and a T-shirt. "Thanks?"

"I just wanted to tell you."

I put my arms around her and kissed her. "I love you, with all my heart. Thank you."

"Come on, I want to get a seat at the bar."

I glanced at the alarm clock on the nightstand. "It's only twelve thirty."

"I know, but you know I like sitting where I can see the TV. I want to get there before it fills up."

Abby was a sports nut. She always wanted to be in front of the big-screen TV so she could watch the latest action, no matter what the sport. "I'm ready."

As I held the door for Abbs outside the restaurant, she practically squealed. "Oh, look! Two seats right up front. Excellent."

We ordered drinks. Abby asked for a draft, while I got a Coke. I was doing a reading at Gabriel's later that evening and didn't want to screw it up by being tipsy or, worse, drunk. I glanced at the menu. "Want to get something? I'm kinda hungry."

"Eat when you get back. You can't be late."

"Jesus, why not? Won't our money be just as good if I'm late, say twenty minutes or so?"

"You can wait and be back here in the same twenty minutes."

"I thought you said quick in and out."

"I'm giving you time to walk across the street and back again...you *are* getting older."

I love Abby with all my heart, but something had the hairs on my neck on end.

"I don't have to ask for anything special, right?"

"Absolutely not. Just let them determine the right size harness and you're out of there."

"Okay. Keep the chair warm for me."

She leaned over and kissed my cheek. "You're my *she*ro."

"Yeah, yeah." I took a deep breath and headed to Wild Hearts.

Outside the store, I took another deep breath and sent up a prayer that no one I knew was inside. I walked in and gasped. Dildos lined the walls, dildos in all shapes, sizes and colors. On the top shelf, a sign announced VIBRATORS OPTIONAL. Another sign declared JUST RIGHT FOR THE G-SPOT. Some were remote control, some glowed in the dark. I didn't know where to look, and everywhere I turned, I was barraged with other sex toys— instruments of lust in all shapes, sizes and, lord help me, for all purposes.

"May I help you?"

I turned to find a child/woman standing before me. "What are you, ten?"

She grinned. "I'm actually twenty-two. Is there something I can help you with?"

"Appointment...I mean, I have an appointment."

"Do you know with whom?" She said the words slowly as if I wouldn't comprehend.

"Yes." I nodded my head.

She smiled at me knowingly. "Do you know her name?"

I nodded again. I did know. "Cheryl. It's Cheryl."

"Good. I'll get her for you. Don't go anywhere."

I shoved my hands in my pockets and tried not to stare at things.

"Hello, I'm Cheryl, can I help you?"

Another child stood before me. This one appeared even younger. "Are you Cheryl?"

"I thought we had established that. Yes, I am."

"I have an appointment."

"And you are?"

I took a ragged breath. "Your one o'clock appointment."

"It's your first time isn't it?" She took my arm and pulled me toward a counter in the front of the store. Once there she opened an appointment book and looked down. "You're Ms. Michaels then?"

"Dani. Dani Michaels."

"See, that wasn't so hard."

I tried to relax, but it was useless. "My wife, she told me you have everything ready, just need to be sure of the size of the belt, right?"

"Belt?"

I felt my cheeks turning red, starting to burn. "Harness, I meant harness."

"Yes. Let's go into the dressing room. That way we can have some privacy."

"Privacy?"

She led me to the back of the store. "Well, I can't very well measure you over your jeans." We had just passed an entire display case of edible clothing—bras, panties, nipple covers. I averted my eyes. Before me stood a rack of ladies' underthings; corsets, lace bras, nippleless bras, satin and lace camisoles and garter sets. On and on it went.

"Right in here. Please take your pants off."

It was futile. I turned beet red. This girl had to be a teenager and she was telling me to take my pants off. I had to be breaking some law.

"Uh, I could do the measurements and just call them out to you."

"Don't be shy, I do this all the time." With that she sat in the chair, staring at me.

I knew my fate had been cast. I unbuckled my belt and opened the button, then slid the zipper downward and stepped out of my jeans. In the mirror I caught a glance at myself. I was wearing my SpongeBob boxers.

"Yes, I can see why your wife was concerned. You do have big thighs."

"Does this mean you can't fit me?"

"Not at all. I just need to get a different size, then I'll bring your purchases in and go over them with you. I'll be just a moment."

Cheryl stepped out of the room, so I grabbed my jeans and slipped them on. I'd be damned if we were going to discuss anything with me undressed.

I was just buckling my belt when she stepped back in.

Cheryl looked at me. "Is something wrong?"

"No."

"Why did you get dressed?"

"You said you knew the size I needed."

Cheryl held up the item in question. "I need to see it on you, show you how to use it, load it. Make sure it's tight enough to hold, but loose enough for comfort."

"Oh." I undid my belt; Sponge-Bob would make another appearance.

"I'd like to suggest a larger size in jeans from now on."

"What? Why?"

"You need to allow room for the harness and accessory."

"Huh?"

"Well, I assumed you'd be wearing it on dates and such, or on special occasions."

"I don't date. I'm married."

"I meant when you and your wife go out."

"In public, you mean?" The room was definitely getting hotter.

"If you went up a size in your jeans, no one would know but you and your lady."

"In public?"

She looked at me pityingly. "Lots of butches do."

Cheryl turned and started unpacking a shopping bag the size of a small minivan.

"The three attachments your wife picked out all work lovely with this belt. As I told her, leather is the way to go. Much sturdier and so many options." Cheryl glanced up and smiled.

"Uh-huh."

"Now this particular one is a favorite of mine." Cheryl removed from the bag what looked like a penis with a long handle attached. *What would...how would. Holy crap, that is not a handle.*

"Your wife was very excited that we had it in stock." Cheryl held up the dual dildo. "This is our best seller. It's called the Nexus. As you can see, the two of you will simultaneously receive enjoyment from this model."

"Uh-huh."

"Here, let's get the harness on you, then I can show you how to load it."

"What?"

"I want to be sure it fits properly. Then we can experiment with the various attachments."

The room was getting warmer and smaller all at once. "Fine."

As Cheryl painstakingly fit the harness over my boxers, she continued her lesson. "Your wife was such a joy to talk to. She had done her research and knew exactly what she was looking for. We spoke on the phone for an hour."

"I'll bet."

"Seriously, you'd be surprised how many women have no idea, and then I have to show and explain all the options." Cheryl tugged on the now-secured harness. "I think that's got it for you. How does it feel?"

"I'm not sure how to answer that."

"It's got to be tight enough to sustain the thrusting motion, but not so tight as to cause chafing or sores."

"We can adjust it, right?"

"Oh, yes, this model is perfect for that."

I looked down, gave it a tug. "Okay, I guess."

Cheryl turned to the table behind her and picked up the Nexus, the double dildo, the mutual satisfaction one. *Crap.*

"Now this one should be inserted this way into the harness first, then be sure to lubricate your end and slip it in as you're tightening the straps on the harness. Shall I demonstrate? I have some lube here."

"No! No...I'll...figure it out, thanks."

She shrugged. "Okay. Just let me show you how to secure the dildo into the harness then. Oh, I better use the other model." She pulled out a shiny pink wobbly one and inserted a battery pack in it. "This is the G-Pulse Dildo attachment. It's battery operated and sure to give you both a little extra sensation. Plus, it's perfect for the G-spot. Also, it's made of soft gel versus the silicone models. It won't last as long, but it's wonderfully soft and pliable, as you can see."

The damn thing was wiggling like a Jell-O mold. I was afraid it would melt.

"Always be sure to get the rim flush against the harness here, see?" She had loosened one strap and inserted the attachment. It now hung in front of me like a body extension.

"How many of these did Abby buy, exactly?"

Cheryl looked up and grinned. "Just one more...another popular one with the femmes. It's called the Bandito. She chose lavender, but she especially liked the contour and shape of that one."

"She did, huh?"

"As I said, your wife was a delight, very knowledgeable. It's a shame she couldn't make the trip with you."

"Yes. Yes, it is." Abby might be a tiger in bed, but she turns red at off-color jokes. On the other hand, she knows her short-comings; this place would be like a candy store to her. She would want to look at everything to learn how it works.

"Now, you're aware that the two silicone models can be put into the dishwasher for sterilization, right? For the soft-gel model we recommend you use prophylactics to ensure cleanliness."

"You mean rubbers?"

"Yes."

I just shook my head. I was going to kill Abby. Kill her dead.

After twenty minutes of me proving I could properly load and unload the various dildos, Cheryl finally let me take off the harness. "We're doing so well. Now have you ever used the Tongue Joy vibrator?"

"I'm almost afraid to ask."

Cheryl chuckled. "It's a vibrator for your tongue."

"Can I get electrocuted?"

"No, it uses batteries and is quite safe and small."

"I'll probably end up swallowing it."

Cheryl just smiled. "Here, let me show you how it works."

"I think I can figure that out. Is there anything else in there?"

"Yes, we still have the video your wife thought you should watch, and I have two models of vibrators she ordered. One for your finger, the Fun Fingazs Vibe; and one she inserts, the Pocket Rocket model."

"Inserts?"

"Yes. Some women like to keep stimulated while working or shopping."

"Is it safe? You know, for a woman to stay stimulated like that?"

"It's wonderful. I have one in right now and love it. So does my wife when I get home, if you know what I mean."

I closed my eyes to the image of children having sex. I now knew I had definitely broken some kind of federal law. I was waiting for the store to be raided and me whisked away in handcuffs.

"So shall we head to the viewing room?"

"The what?"

"It's where you can watch the video in comfort. Afterward you can ask me questions and I'll answer them for you."

"I can't believe I'm going to ask this, but what kind of video is this?"

Cheryl gave me a patronizing smile. "An instructional one, though we do have others if you're interested in that kind of thing."

"No. No, that's fine. In fact I think I'll let my wife watch the video with me, and if she has any questions she can always call you later, right?"

"Of course. I'll take this up front. When you're ready, come to the counter and I'll ring you up."

After she left, I banged my head on the wall three or four times. I could not believe Abby had set me up. She knew. She knew and still she sent me in here alone. I slipped back into my jeans and headed to the front of the store.

When I stepped outside, I took a deep breath. My insides were shaking and I was more determined to kill Abby then ever. I was now saddled with a small human-size shopping bag that had the name of the boutique emblazoned in red letters across it. I looked both ways, trying to figure out what to do, where to stash the bag.

I trotted into the restaurant. Abby was engrossed in a football game and cheering along with the other women alongside her. I walked up and placed the bag on the bar. "Here's your purchases, sweetie."

Abby turned, saw the name on the bag, and grabbed it off the countertop. "Are you crazy?"

I smiled. "No, baby, I just wanted you to have the full experience." I sat down next to her and let her deal with the satchel.

Abby looked at me from the corner of her eye, trying to hide the bag between her and the wall. "You're mad?"

"Nope."

"What took so long?"

"As if you don't know?"

She turned to face me, her expression blank. "I don't."

"Don't lie, sweetheart, Cheryl gave you up."

Now it was Abby's turn to blush. "I'm really not sure what you mean."

"Let me explain it." Just then Jillian, the bartender, stepped up. "Another Coke please, and some wings for two." I turned back to Abby, lowered my voice. "Not only did Cheryl have to measure me, but then she proceeded to strap me in and demonstrate how every fucking thing you bought is used."

Abby tried to smother her laughter.

"I'm not amused Abbs."

"She really demonstrated it. Everything?"

"Oh, yeah." My temper finally kicked in. "I can honestly say I feel quite confident that I can pack any dildo into the harness without a hitch, that I know exactly how to wash and care for the models you purchased—three, is that right? I also am positive that I know how and where the tongue and finger vibrators go and how to use them. We have lubricants in three flavors, all water-based, and I know that the raspberry flavor is the most natural-tasting one. I am assured you will be safe stimulating yourself while out in public with your little Pocket Rocket...oh, and I need to buy bigger jeans. How's that for a synopsis?"

Too late, I realized my voice had risen in my fervor to make Abby understand my complete and total mortification. I hadn't paid attention to the fact that the volume on the TVs had been muted, that all eyes of the other patrons were on us, or that Jillian was there with our appetizers.

A thunderous round of applause broke out at the bar as I concluded my speech. Abby did what I had wanted to do earlier; she ran out of the bar as fast as she could, leaving me to carry the bag back to the hotel room.

"Oh. My. God."

I lifted my head and smiled up from between Abby's legs.

"That was the best sex ever."

I swiped my tongue one more time up through her folds, then climbed up next to her and kissed her on the lips. "Pretty good, huh?"

Abby grinned. "Better than good, perfect."

I rolled over and pulled her snug up against me.

Abby nuzzled my neck. "Feeling pretty good about yourself, aren't you?"

"Absolutely. And it was all me, no damn gadgets."

Abby laughed out loud. "Yes it was, and it was wonderful."

"See, I told you we didn't need this stuff."

"I'm sorry I laughed."

"Yeah, well, I guess if you didn't know what to expect, it was a little silly-looking."

"It was as if it had a life of its own."

"I guess I didn't tighten it enough. But you didn't need to laugh."

"You looked so miserable."

"It's not that bad, just takes some getting used to, I guess."

Abby started caressing my chest. "Does that mean you're willing to try again?"

"Not if you're going to laugh."

"I promise not to, not now that I know how it looks." She kissed me. "Please?"

"I guess. It's not like I have to go shopping. We already have everything...might as well get our money's worth."

Abby sat up. "Come on, I'll help you this time. You can show me what you learned."

"Now?"

"Yes, now."

"But we just did it."

"And now we're going to do it again."

"Twice in one day?" I looked at her incredulously. "At our age?"

"Do you feel old right now?"

I jumped up and went across the room where I had flung the harness. "So which model do you want tonight, my dear?"

"Let's try the Bandito, shall we?"

"You had to get the lavender one...you couldn't get the black one?"

"Are you going to complain or put it to use?"

"I can't wait to have your mother find one of these in the dishwasher."

ABOUT THE AUTHORS

MICHELLE BRENNAN is a queer artistic Pisces who likes to cause a ruckus in the Midwest with her surly butch unicorn and their gang of feral kitties. With an imagination too big to fit into a bread box, she can't help but write dirty stories and incite desire and sexy adventures for the masses.

AMY BUTCHER is exactly that and when she isn't wrestling with the responsibilities of that twist of nomenclatural destiny she writes, facilitates workshops and does massage in San Francisco. Her murder mystery *Paws for Consideration* was published in 2011. Find her at amybutcher.com.

DEBORAH CASTELLANO (deborahmcastellano.com) made her erotica debut in Violet Blue's *Best Women's Erotica 2009*. She is a freelance and romantica writer by trade and also blogs about kitchen witchcraft and radical practicality.

DEJAY's work has appeared in anthologies by Bedazzled Ink, as well as in *Lesbian Cowboys* and *Lesbian Lust: Erotic Stories* (Cleis). Her books include *Redemption* and *Strangers*. DeJay and her lovely wife of thirty-three years live in the mountains of Pennsylvania when they are not traveling around the U.S. in their RV. Contact: dejaynovl.org.

LEA DELARIA, the first openly queer comic to perform on television in America, has starred in two Broadway musicals and has five records out on the Warner Jazz label. Lea has an Obie and Theater World award, has twice been honored by the Drama League and her book *Lea's Book of Rules for the World* is in its third printing.

KIKI DELOVELY is a queer femme performer/writer whose work has appeared in *Best Lesbian Erotica 2011*; *Salacious* magazine, *She's Gotta Have It: 69 Stories of Sudden Sex; Take Me There: Transgender and Genderqueer Erotica* and *Say Please: Lesbian BDSM Erotica*. Kiki's passions include artichokes, words, alternative baking and taking on research for her writing.

JULIA NOEL GOLDMAN is a native New Yorker, a political activist and a graduate of Sarah Lawrence College. Her lesbian erotica has been translated into Russian, French and Spanish, and is available on the Internet. This is her first story to be published in an anthology. Find out more at julianoelgoldman.com.

ILY GOYANES is a Latina lesbian who lives to learn. When she isn't writing for the *Miami New Times* newspaper, she likes to get dirty in her kitchen and in bed. Her fictional debut appeared in *Lesbian Cops* (Cleis). Visit thesideshow.info and share your most sinful recipe.

ANNE GRIP lives in New York City with her girlfriend. She is a newly beginning yoga practitioner.

NANCY IRWIN is an out, queer, S/M activist. She has given sex and S/M workshops locally and internationally, organized events and play parties and published articles in the queer and kinky press. Nancy is a street biker who loves the dirt and a bad dyke who plays well with "others." A Leather Pride flag marks her Toronto home.

Editor of *Carnal Machines, Spank, The Sweetest Kiss* and the Lammy Finalist, *Where the Girls Are*, find **D. L. KING'**s stories in *Best Lesbian Erotica, Best Women's Erotica, Girl Crazy* and *Broadly Bound*, among others. She's published two novels and edits the review site, Erotica Revealed. Find her at dlkingerotica.com.

LULU LAFRAMBOISE is a fantasy name, so in this fantasy life, Lulu leads dive excursions in Belize and studies the rainbow parrotfish. In real life, Lulu writes serious nonfiction and teaches creative writing at an Ivy League university.

KIRSTY LOGAN lives in Glasgow, Scotland with her very own rebel girl. She writes in *The Rumpus, Filthy Gorgeous Things, Best Lesbian Erotica 2011* and *Best Women's Erotica 2011*. She has a semicolon tattooed on her toe. Say hello at kirstylogan.com.

DANI M (danim251@gmail.com) is a journalist and magazine editor who creates erotica to honor and contribute to the art and expression of lesbian sexuality, in a world that rarely represents us. She gives thanks to the amazing women who have inspired her writing. Dani lives with her special one, H, in London.

EVAN MORA's tales of sex, cars and other passions have appeared in many fine publications including: *Best Lesbian Erotica '09, Best Lesbian Romance '09* and *'10, Where the Girls Are, Girl Crush, Lesbian Cops* and *Daddy's Little Girl: Butch/Femme Erotica.* She lives in Toronto.

ALI OH has a taste for sex, humor and grammar. Aside from her computer equipment, her sex toy box is the object in the house with the highest monetary value. She can be found running around New Jersey with her girlfriend or at madeofwords.com. Because the sexiest stuff is made of words.

Eroticist **GISELLE RENARDE** (wix.com/gisellerenarde/erotica) is a queer Canadian, contributor to dozens of short-story anthologies, an avid volunteer and author of numerous electronic and print books. Ms. Renarde lives across from a park with two bilingual cats who sleep on her head.

TREASURE SAPPHIRE is a former phone sex operator and full-time sex kitten operating out of Fort Lauderdale. She enjoys engaging in unethical acts of depraved debauchery and leaping tall buildings in a single bound. A self-proclaimed "drag hag," she delights in gender play and has several titillating alter egos. Find her at treasures.pleasure.chest@gmail.com.

ELENA SHEARIN is a new writer of lesbian erotica though she has been a longtime reader and fan. This is her first publication and she is excited about the opportunity to introduce her writing to other people. She welcomes feedback at elena.shearin@gmail.com.

SHARON WACHSLER lives in rural New England. Her lesborotica is in dozens of magazines and anthologies, including *Best Lesbian Erotica 2003* and *2009*, and *Best American Erotica 2004* and *2005*. The Astraea Foundation has named Sharon an Emerging Lesbian Fiction Writer. Sharon blogs about writing, service-dog training, and disability at aftergadget.wordpress.com.

ANNA WATSON is a married old-school femme mom. More of her stories are in *Sometimes She Lets Me*, *Girl Crazy*, *BLE '07, '08, '09, Fantasy: Untrue Stories of Lesbian Passion* and *Take Me There*. She also has an essay about being a femme book-worm in *Visible: A Femmethology, Volume One*.

XAN WEST is the pseudonym of an NYC BDSM/sex educator. Xan's "First Time Since," won honorable mention for the 2008 NLA John Preston Short Fiction Award. Xan has appeared in many anthologies, including *Best SM Erotica 2* and *3*, *Best Women's Erotica 2008* and *2009* and *Best Lesbian Erotica 2011*.

ABOUT THE EDITORS

KATHLEEN WARNOCK is a playwright, fiction writer and editor. Her erotica has appeared (under the name Kyle Walker) in *Best Lesbian Erotica, A Woman's Touch, Best Lesbian Romance* and *Friction 7,* among others. Her fiction, essays and reviews have been seen in *ROCKRGRL, BUST, Ms., Metal Maidens, It's Only Rock and Roll, Gargoyle, American Book Review, New Directions for Women* and the liner notes for the Joan Jett CD *Unfinished Business.* Her plays have been produced in New York, the United Kingdom and regionally. *Rock the Line* (published by United Stages) was produced by Emerging Artists Theatre in New York and won the Robert Chesley Award for Emerging Playwright. *Grieving for Genevieve* won the John Golden Award for Playwriting. *Some Are People* won the Arts & Letters Award for Drama. She is curator of the Robert Chesley/ Jane Chambers Playwrights Project for TOSOS Theater, and Playwrights Company Manager for Emerging Artists Theater. She is Ambassador of Love for the International Dublin Gay

Theatre Festival and a member of the Dramatists Guild. Find her online at kathleenwarnock.com, Twitter: @kwarnockny.

SINCLAIR SEXSMITH (mrsexsmith.com) writes the award-winning personal online project *Sugarbutch Chronicles: The Sex, Gender, and Relationship Adventures of a Kinky Queer Butch Top* at sugarbutch.net, and has works published in various anthologies, including the *Best Lesbian Erotica 2011, 2009, 2007* and *2006* collections; *Sometimes She Lets Me: Best Butch/ Femme Erotica; Visible: A Femmethology Volume II; Persistence: All Ways Butch and Femme; Take Me There: Transgender and Genderqueer Erotica,* and more. She is a regular columnist for AfterEllen.com, LambdaLiterary.org and SexIsMagazine. com and has written for GoodVibes Magazine, GoMagazine. com, and CarnalNation.com. She has released three chapbooks of poetry, one chapbook of smut, and one spoken word CD. Her first erotica anthology, *Say Please: Lesbian BDSM Erotica,* releases in 2012 from Cleis Press.

Mr. Sexsmith holds degrees in both gender studies and creative writing, studied and taught at Bent Writing Institute for queers in Seattle, and currently teaches community and academic workshops on gender, sexuality, chivalry, healing, communication, and getting the sex life you want. Monthly in her current home of New York City, she coproduces Sideshow: Queer Literary Carnival reading series. She prefers the pronouns she/her as well as the masculine honorific of "Mr." In her spare time, she likes to cook, read, swing dance, sip whiskey, and look at the stars.